GRIGORI

A Medieval Fantasy

CIRCLE OF ASSASSINS

ANN GIMPEL

CONTENTS

GRIGORI

CIRCLE OF ASSASSINS, BOOK FIVE

Medieval Fantasy

By
Ann Gimpel

Tumble off reality's edge into a twisted world fueled by lore and magic

Copyright Page

BOOK DESCRIPTION, GRIGORI

I like things neat, so shoot me. Or poison me. Or run me through with a broadsword. Doesn't matter how you try to end me, werewolves are immortal.

Back to liking things neat... I've been killing forever, both as a wolf and as a man. The assassin trade has always been lucrative, and, a few hundred years back, a much simpler affair. No DNA tests. No sophisticated crime labs. I didn't have to plan the way I do today to avoid detection.

Not that it would matter if I were apprehended. I'd just vanish to a borderworld for a while and resurface once the heat died down. Mostly, I deal with supernatural enemies these days. Keeps things cleaner.

But this book isn't about today. It's about long ago. I've done my damnedest to instill pride and standards into the assassin trade. And bond animals. Their principles definitely add class to the mix.

Building the Circle was an uphill battle. I almost gave up more times than I can count, but nothing worthwhile comes easy. The Circle of Assassins became my life's work. Didn't plan it that way, but life happens. Life, bloodthirsty mages, and the bond animals who adore them.

Author note: This book can be read as a standalone, but for the best experience, you might want to read the first four books in this series.

BOOKS IN THE CIRCLE OF ASSASSINS SERIES:

AUTHOR'S NOTE

Between Covid-19 and the California fires, I've had a lot of time to dream up ideas for books. Watching too much *Blacklist* and *Warehouse 13* and *Stranger Things* probably didn't help. And the last season of *Supernatural*. I will miss Sam and Dean...

Meanwhile, a concept shaped up for me. Assassins have always held a fascination factor. Death is a job for them, but what kind of people are they beneath their knives and guns and poison? Toss a few bond animals into the mix, and the bones for a darkish urban fantasy series took shape.

Within its pages, you'll ride alongside men and women who found their way to an age-old profession. Every king worth his salt had a court assassin, and so has every ruler from olden times to modern. If you're shaking your head saying such things can't happen today, take a look at "suicides" and "accidents" that are swept under a whole bunch of rugs.

Oddly enough, all those suspicious deaths had stories to tell, stories someone wanted silenced—forever.

Grigori formed the Circle of Assassins centuries ago. This is his story, the why and how of the Circle. It reads well as a standalone, but be sure to check out the other four books in this series too.

dinburgh Castle, 1542

"Bring Grigori to me now!" James V thundered.

I bared my teeth in a snarl. I'd been avoiding the bastard who ruled Scotland for a while now, but my werewolf hearing is acute. James's command reverberated, reaching my perch under the castle's eaves. He'd come to the throne at the tender age of seventeen months in 1513. Since he'd been king his whole life, he'd never learned much of anything. His tantrums were legion. Even though he'd passed the threshold of adulthood years ago, his juvenile behavior never altered.

I shook myself and completed my transformation to my human form. All that crap about werewolves only claiming their wolf bodies during a full moon was made up by a bunch of superstitious fools. Any werewolf worth his salt can change shape any time.

Still, I didn't flaunt my other body. It would only get in

the way of my status in James's court. Worse, the church advisors would demand my head and place James in an untenable position. He knows what I am, but it's not a topic we ever discuss.

Slaps and blows followed the king's orders. Guess his minions weren't moving quickly enough to suit him. It decided me. Not that I had friends in the court. Everyone gives assassins a wide berth. Still, others suffering on my account has never set well.

I dragged on a pair of leather breeks and stout hobnail boots. My hair was loose, my chest bare, but it would have to do. As turned out as I was likely to be, I entered the convoluted series of secret passageways that meandered through the castle.

I didn't build them, but I added keyholes in prime locations to make spying simpler. James would be shocked by how many supernaturals frequented his halls. Most, like Leprechauns and Brownies, were harmless, but the occasional vampire sauntered through. Demons too.

They know what I am, which is why I use keyholes rather than magic to snoop. Helps maintain an element of surprise before I pounce.

After a quick peek at a deserted hallway on the castle's main floor, I slithered out of a rotating bookshelf system taking care to seal it into place. It would never do for one of the urchins roving the castle's halls to stumble onto my passageways by accident.

James had produced a score of illicit brats. I'm not against children, but I prefer them well-behaved, a joke around here. Assuming the queen's current pregnancy continued uninterrupted, James was finally on the brink of producing a legitimate heir. If that happened, all the young wannabes would become far less visible. Sometimes, bastards met with unfortunate accidents.

Would I be the instrument of their destruction?

Unlikely since I draw the line at snuffing out mortal children.

I rounded corner after corner, moving at a decent clip but stopping shy of an actual trot. I might work for James, but I viewed the relationship as one of equals. I did his dirty work for fair compensation.

The day he disrespected me like he did most everyone else would be the day I walked away and found some other regent to work for. Freelancing held a definite appeal too.

I entered the day room, where the king conducted most of his business, and stopped a meter inside the doorway. He wasn't paying any attention. Big surprise since one of his nubile nymphs, this one exceedingly young, knelt between his legs. I could have waited until she was done.

Could have. A perverse part of me delighted in raising my voice. "You were hunting me, my liege?"

James's head popped up. His eyes snapped open.

Courtiers lining both sides of the room hustled forward to snatch the maid away and rearrange James's velveteen robes.

"Where have you been?" He eyed me with annoyance. "You could have waited. You saw I was otherwise engaged."

I shrugged. "Thought you needed me. I'll be on my way."

I hadn't gone two steps before he screeched, "I did not dismiss you."

So that's how it was going to be.

Turning, I balanced on the balls of my feet and stared

right at him. A big faux pas, but I didn't care. My time was as important as his, even if he didn't see it that way.

"How is that project coming?" he asked.

I riffled through my memory and didn't identify any work I hadn't yet completed. "Everything has been attended to." I didn't tack "my liege," onto the end of my sentence on purpose.

He surged to his feet and banged the end of a long silver scepter on the polished hardwood floor. "Then why did I just see Lord Willoughby in these very corridors yesterday?"

After more memory riffling, I came up with a rather weak vampire who'd presented in James's court the previous week.

"What about him?" I asked, certain he hadn't been one of my assignments.

"Leave us!" James spread his arms wide. He's a piss-poor specimen for a human. Perhaps a meter-and-a-half tall and skinny as an underfed horse, he had shoulder-length thinning black hair, a pointed beard, and bloodshot dark eyes. If he'd lay off the liquor, his mind might be sharper.

Today, his velvet robe was a deep-ruby color sashed in cream. Rings clanked on every finger, and an enormous emerald hung around his neck from a thick golden chain. I've warned him about that chain. Someone could use it to choke the life out of him.

Of course, he didn't listen.

The courtiers and their underlings filed from the throne room. The maid had vanished a while back. Once everyone was gone, I shut the door and walked closer to the king.

His sudden need for secrecy was amusing. Everyone knew what purpose I served for the court, even if they pretended otherwise. And James had already identified my next victim.

It would be telling if Willoughby was still around when I looked for him.

If he wasn't, James had a mole in his ranks, something I'd long suspected. Much like my advice regarding his neck chain, he'd also ignored my suggestion his inner circle might not be totally loyal.

"Sire?" I met his gaze, didn't bother dropping to one knee or any of the other crap.

"I told you to get rid of him," he snarled in a stage whisper.

"If you say so." I aimed for neutral since he'd done no such thing.

"Go." He flapped his hands my way. "Don't return until it's done."

Usually, I don't tolerate him talking to me that way. Today, I let it slide because I had a different agenda. "Willoughby won't bother you again. In return, I require Inverness Castle."

His mouth gaped open and shut like a landed fish. "You require?" he sputtered. "Who are you to talk thusly to us?"

I shrugged. "Your royal assassin? The only one in your court you can truly trust. Is there some problem with that particular castle?"

"Only that it's occupied by George Gordon, Fourth Earl of Huntley. He's been rebuilding it, but it won't be done for another few years. The place was an eyesore. I'm grateful someone rose to the task."

Of course, I knew all that. The castle's partially finished state, plus the fact it straddled a gateway to borderworlds made it attractive to me.

I waited, holding the king's gaze. More words wouldn't

help. He knew what I wanted, and what I was willing to trade to get it.

"It would be cheaper to hire this out elsewhere," he muttered.

"Not necessarily."

"What do you mean? I know you, Grigori. Speak plainly. Do not make me dig the truth out of a pile of fancy words."

Truth, eh. Alrighty. "Willoughby is a vampire. If you don't rid the court of him, you run the risk of an incursion. These things are far simpler when you get a jump on them."

James raised his upper lip in a sneer. "How do you know?"

"Takes one to know one, in a manner of speaking."

"Pfft. No wonder I distrusted the man. Fine. Do what you must."

"Inverness Castle?" I pressed to ensure it would be mine once I delivered the goods.

"I'll work on it."

"Not good enough."

"No one talks to us in that fashion."

I refrained from pointing out I just did and waited. He was repeating himself, a sure sign he was nervous. I had all the time in the world, or at least until nightfall, which was hours away. Wiping out vamps during daylight was ridiculously simple. All I had to do was find his coffin—or wherever he'd gone to ground—and rip the lid off it.

Sunlight kills them. No need for fancy silver stakes.

"Fine. Deal." James sounded sullen.

"Deal. I will reach out when I'm done," I told him and walked away. If it had been anyone but the king, I'd have sealed his promise with a blood bond, but even I knew which lines not to cross.

I made my way back to my quarters under the castle's eaves. This time, I traveled via stairways and corridors as I plotted out the most unobtrusive way to deal with Willoughby.

He had to be part of a seethe. Vampires never travel alone. I had an arrangement with the local one. Or rather, a détente. I let them be, and vice versa. Willoughby might be visiting them, or he might not be affiliated in any way.

Regardless, the seethe would be my first stop. Depending on what I discovered, I'd move forward from there. I'd reached the short set of stairs leading to my room. Halfway up, I noticed my door standing open.

I hadn't left it that way.

Power flowed around me in protective waves as I loped to the top step ready to flatten whoever had the temerity to show up unannounced. My chamber sat empty.

What the unholy hell?

I stopped at the threshold and reached out with seeking threads. I needn't have been so cautions. Dragon essence filled my room. Explained why it was empty. No dragon over the age of six months would have fit in my cozy space. Crossing the room in half a dozen paces, I stared out the window.

Sure enough, a silver dragon with reddish wings rode the updrafts high overhead, wings pumping and furling as the mood struck her.

Aidyrth, elder dragon, and a friend, was bonded with a water mage.

Raising a hand, I waved. *"Well met. What can I do for you today?"*

"There you are," she bugled. *"I knew that open door would get your attention."*

Back in the 1500s, dragons weren't uncommon sights. Humans revered them, left offerings of sheep, goats, and cows. The dragons never wasted so much as a hoof.

"Here I am," I agreed cheerfully. Something about dragons soothes the soul, or sets it on fire with longing for the unimaginable. For a time when magic was pure and untainted. When mortals hadn't sullied the world with their plotting and greed.

"Meet me in the field north of the castle," she bugled and wheeled, wings cutting cleanly through the air.

I crafted a quick journey spell to save time and emerged about the same moment she skidded in for a landing.

"You must come." Fire and ash streamed from her open jaws.

"Where and why?"

"Cornwall. There have been more botched assassinations. This time, they're bad enough the townspeople are outraged and have marched on the duke. He's walled up in his castle."

"He's who ordered the assassinations, right?"

She shook her head until scales rattled. "Nay. Another masquerading under the royal seal ordered them. It's such a mess. Gives us all a bad name."

"Where's Delilah?" I asked. The water mage had been bonded with Aidyrth for many a long year. I'd never seen them apart before.

"In Cornwall," she replied in tense tones.

"Out with it. What happened?" I leaned closer, breathing in the baked-clay smell of her.

"The duke singled her out and is blaming her for

everything. She's in the dungeon, and I can't get her out." Aidyrth tilted her head back and blew a gout of flame skyward.

Before she could ask again, I said, "Of course, I'll help you, but first, there's a pesky vampire I need to do away with."

She dropped her head onto my shoulder. "How long will that take?"

"Only a few hours if things go well."

"I could help. I hate those undead monsters."

"Let me start with the local seethe to see what they know, and—"

"You have a relationship with those abominations?" Aidyrth sounded horrified. She jerked her head upward, no longer touching me.

"Don't get your scales ruffled. Nothing that fancy. But they've never done me wrong. Sometimes, they have information I can't get elsewhere."

"Why can't the vampire wait?" More flames scudded skyward.

"Because James is gifting me a castle."

If a dragon could look surprised, Aidyrth did. She flapped her wings, fanning heated air my way. "What do you want with such a thing?"

"I'm not sure yet, but I've learned to roll with my instincts. It straddles a gateway to borderworlds and could be useful." I blew out a breath. "Where will you be?"

"Around. Do not make me wait too long."

I mimed a salute. "Don't worry, Madam Dragon, I wouldn't dream of it. Delilah is tough. We'll get her out of there."

"We'd better, or I'll burn down the world."

She wasn't kidding. Dragon wrath is legendary. I've never been on its receiving end, and I'd like to keep it that way.

I took off running. The local vamps would be far more inclined to hear me out if I showed up at their crypt and knocked politely than if I teleported inside with no warning.

Pays to know your enemies, and I made a habit of doing just that.

Edinburgh has many cemeteries. Naturally, vampires had picked the oldest one and set up shop in a multilevel crypt that had once been the purview of the MacLind clan. Its few surviving members had protested vigorously and were given the choice of death or assimilation.

Not that I follow these things closely, but if memory serves they all signed on with the rest of the undead.

It took about half an hour to cover the distance to the cemetery. I'd have been quicker in wolf form, much quicker, but it was broad daylight. A wolf racing down the city streets would have drawn the wrong kind of attention. I'm impervious to arrows, but not falling on my side in death throes would have posed its own set of problems.

The clergy employ sorcerers. While they acknowledged dragons, even respected them, werewolves weren't afforded that luxury. I did not need anything slowing me down. Not today with Delilah imprisoned in Cornwall.

I crossed the rough stone wall separating graves from cobblestone streets and made my way across a stream. The door to the MacLind crypt had been rebuilt since I was last here. New lumber provided a stark contrast to everything else in this sector of the graveyard.

It surprised me. One of the first things supernatural beings learn is to maintain a very low profile. While the undead MacLinds had pretended nothing changed, it only worked for a decade or so. After that, they staged their deaths to avoid difficult explanations for questions such as why they weren't getting any older.

I've run into much the same problem. Every few years, I change venues, create a new backstory, and return to my preferred trade as an assassin. I hadn't actually been here when the last MacLind went to ground, but I'd gotten an earful from a gossipy Brownie.

The crypt door swung open. "We know you're out there, Grigori," a voice issued from within.

I strode forward, stopping before the lintel. "May I enter?"

"My, so formal." A familiar chuckle followed the words.

"Logan?"

"The same, mate. If you don't get in here soon, though, I'm closing the door."

I hustled through; the heavy door slammed shut leaving me in a dimly lit room lined with more new lumber. "Why the renovation project?" I swung an arm wide.

Logan drew back his upper lip in a snarl that displayed yellowed fangs. He's one of the older vamps in this seethe. Means he can tolerate a brush of sunlight without dying, which might explain why he drew sentry duty.

Medium height with a beefy build, he had rust-colored curls, amber eyes, and a square chin covered with stubble. They remain the same after they're turned, not aging or changing in any elemental way. Usually, they don't bother with garments unless they leave the seethe, but Logan sported a tartan that hung to his knees in a black, green, and gold pattern. The upper portion was wrapped around his shoulders.

"Local hooligans amused themselves by looting this part of the graveyard," he said in answer to my question.

"Ha. Bet they got a shred more than they bargained for,"

"You might say so. We weren't on the lookout for recruits, but they've provided many a meal. Some still are."

It was more information than I needed. Despite knowing vampires kept stables of mortals for food, the practice has always disgusted me. I'm all about clean kills, not draining my victims until they're almost dead, bringing them back, and doing it again.

"What brings you here?" Logan went on. "Not like you to engage in social calls."

"You know me too well."

"Not well enough." His eyes gleamed in the low light of the boxy room. "We could do something about that lapse."

I stared him down. "Not in this lifetime or any other."

"Be a sport. Just a taste? Werewolf blood is rumored to be ambrosial."

"You asked why I'm here." I purposely changed the subject. "A Lord Willoughby has been lurking around the court. James wants him dead. Is he one of yours?"

Logan frowned, furrows forming between his russet

eyebrows. "Never heard of him. Are you certain he's one of us?"

"Quite sure."

"That's disturbing. We all know the rules."

We all might, but I didn't. "What rules?"

"When we leave our home seethe, we're to check in with any seethe we pass during our journey."

"Does it mean you all know where every seethe is?"

He nodded.

The foray into vampire culture was intriguing, but I had everything I needed. No one in this seethe would give a crap what happened to Willoughby.

"Thanks, Logan. I'll be on my way."

"Not so fast." A beefy hand lashed out and grabbed my forearm.

"Let go," I growled, the transformation to wolf well underway. Before it went any further, I redirected a jot of magic to get my clothes out of the way.

Interest kindled in the depths of his eyes. "Incredible. Shapeshifters aren't nearly as quick."

By then, little was left of my man's body. I curled my jaws around the hand still gripping my foreleg. *"Let go or lose your hand."*

It was an empty threat. Vampires taste horrible. Biting him was a last resort, but he didn't know that.

"Where'd your sense of humor go?" he groused, but he did unhand me.

"Not sure I ever had one," I said after I'd shifted and pulled my garments back into place. "Do not do that again."

"Noted," he said dryly and half bowed. "You're free to go,

but we could take care of Lord Willoughby for you. Evading our laws carries its own set of consequences."

"Do they include actual death?"

A corner of his mouth twitched revealing a fang tip. "No, but James doesn't have to know. Willoughby would vanish from sight. It's kind of the same thing."

The offer was tempting, particularly since it didn't appear to come with strings. Still, James had tasked me with Willoughby's demise, and Inverness Castle hung in the balance. James had been reluctant to deed it to me. If I reported that vampires had dealt with one of their own, he might glom onto it as a reason to welch.

I could lie, but James has spies everywhere. I pride myself on impeccable credibility. If I said Willoughby was dead, he needed to be just that: dead.

"I'll think about it," I told the vampire and left the crypt. Rain pelted down from leaden skies, the contrast a welcome change from the stifling funk inside. Vampires have a particular odor. Humans probably can't smell the faint tinge of decay that clings to them, but my senses are acute.

I didn't have to think about anything, even though I'd used it as an excuse to exit the seethe. My next task was to locate Willoughby. It would have been simpler to return to the court and wait for him to show up that evening. Then I could track him and discover the location of his lair.

That approach would require a whole extra day, if I waited for the next sunrise to unmake him. I inhaled briskly. Even an additional twelve hours was far too long.

Aidyrth was waiting. I'd promised her I'd make quick work of my latest assignment, and I stay true to my word. Methodical as always, I moved from one sector of the city to the next, hunting vampire spoor. I looked in all the obvious places before moving to more remote possibilities.

The day shifted from morning to noon to midafternoon with me no closer to locating my target than I'd been when I walked out of the seethe. I stopped at an outdoor cart to buy mead and biscuits stuffed with mutton.

What was I missing?

Had someone in the court tipped him off? My mole theory was looking more and more likely.

It's one thing to be right, another to be efficient.

I raised my mind voice. *"Aidyrth?"*

"Still here. What's keeping you?"

"Can't find the vampire."

Rolling dragon laughter blasted through my head, rattling my brains. *"I just did. He's under your nose. You're slipping, Grigori. Badly."*

"Define under my nose." Her comment stung, but I'd take all the help I could get. Besides, she said she'd only just located him, which meant she'd been searching the whole day as well.

"In the castle subcellar, northwest wing."

I slapped my forehead with a palm. Nothing like hiding in plain view. He'd picked a spot that wasn't frequented until evening. By then, it would be safe for him to show his undead face aboveground.

Except this time, there'd be no more showing anything anywhere.

"I'd have taken care of him myself, but I don't fit in such close spaces," the dragon bugled. *"Was just about to call you, but you found me."*

Gratitude dug its claws into me. Dragons can be unspeakably arrogant, but she'd been generous with her knowledge. She could just as easily have watched me flounder about hunting for a solution. Of course, she had ulterior motives. Worry for Delilah must be eating at her.

"Thank you."

"Pay me back by hurrying," she prodded.

A quick glance at the sky told me I was running out of time. Dusk would fall in less than an hour. I ducked between a couple of crumbling buildings and set a spell to take me to the castle cellars. The moment my casting cleared—and I took pains to ward myself—I smelled vampire.

Moldy. Musty. Saturated with rot. And far stronger than usual vampire odors. The wine cellars were down this corridor. They provided good cover since anyone passing by would assume a cask had developed a leak—or gone bad.

No one else was down here. I shed my clothes and shifted. Undressing is always better than using magic to get my garments out of the way. I got lucky in the seethe. Often as not, when I take shortcuts like that, my garments end up ripped and ruined.

I jettisoned my ward and hoped Willoughby was down for a nap. Wards shield my presence and cloak most of my magic, but they're nearly impossible to fight through.

Nostrils twitching, I scented the air and glided nearer to my target. I didn't have anything fancy planned. Fancy went along with my human form. Once I got close, I'd spring and rip out the big vessels in his neck. After he'd bled out enough to lose consciousness, I'd grab a silver stake from the castle armory and finish the job.

It would take days to get the reek of vampire blood out of my fur, but it couldn't be helped. And the flavor out of my mouth. They taste abysmal.

Silent on my big pads, I glided down the passageway, stopping in front of each door to sniff. While Willoughby's scent was thick in the passage, I didn't sense it in any of the side chambers.

Made no sense. He had to have holed up somewhere.

All of a sudden, I couldn't smell him anymore. Not at all.

The guard hairs rose on my neck and along my back.

Something significant had altered. I knew it in my guts, but I had no idea what changed. The tunnel was the same. I'd trod this path beneath the castle hundreds of times. Today, it was different.

Had I walked into a trap?

Don't see how. No one knew I'd be here except the dragon. She's on my side.

I slipped through a partially open door and into a room lined with shelves and wine casks lying on their sides. My nostrils twitched faster as the acrid bite of poison slammed into me.

Poison.

Was someone planning to get rid of James?

It happens, and far more frequently than you'd believe. He'd led the country into one unpopular war after another. It made him a prime target.

With no warning, something slammed into me from behind, knocking me into a shelf. Casks rolled off it, breaking open and filling the room with the heady scent of raw spirits. I pivoted sideways, magic running wide open as I made sense of what just happened.

A board peppered with nails swiped me from one side. It would have done more damage if my reflexes weren't so finely honed. I see well in the dark; still I needed better light if I was to defend myself. A small window sat high on one wall. Leaping, I ripped the paper coating off it. Dingy gray illumination spilled through the once-neat space.

Casks rolled every which way. A hollow pounding drew me toward the door. Ha. Someone was nailing it shut.

Nice try.

Werewolves have preternatural strength, but even I needed three tries to splinter the stout boards. They gave way with a clatter. I vaulted over the wreckage after a fleeing figure. It might be Willoughby or not, but fury swelled through me. No one takes me on and wins.

No one.

The man had a head start, but I'm faster than damn near anything on two legs or four. Banking on it being the vampire, I closed the distance between us, but not all the way.

Chivvying my enemy this way and that, I herded him toward the inevitable: a door leading to the outside. Of course, it opened onto a set of steps sunken into the earth, but daylight was daylight. To save my opponent the harsh choice of whether to open the door or not, I sent a jolt of magic to open it for him.

He had no option but to stagger through.

I waited until he was halfway up the steps to pounce. He was done for. We both knew it. I wanted fear to get her teeth into him before I finished him off. I know what I said about clean kills, but Willoughby had led me on a merry chase, and I intended for him to suffer.

If it was him.

I had yet to see his face.

Still, whoever writhed beneath my body smelled like a vampire. How many could there be? Willoughby had only been here a handful of days. Turning minions takes time, and newly minted vampires are almost unmanageable from blood hunger.

It's one reason their seethe structure makes sense and provides a safe place for brand-new vampires to do something other than running amok biting every mortal who crosses their path.

Fangs narrowly missed one of my paws.

That did it. I rolled the man over and bent his back, cracking vertebrae against the stone steps. The sun chose that moment to filter down the stairway illuminating Willoughby's blond perfection just before his skin blistered and turned black.

I turned my head away. Vampire reek was mixed with the poison I'd smelled earlier. Nightshade. It wouldn't have harmed the vampire. What was he doing with it?

I shook him by the shoulders. *"Who were you going to poison?"* I shouted into his mind. He wasn't so far gone he couldn't answer, but he remained stubbornly silent.

"Tell me, and I'll bring you back." It was a boldfaced lie, but maybe he was so desperate it would work.

"Since when are werewolves healers?" His mind voice was scratchy, weak, and laced with bitter humor.

Flesh crumbled beneath my fingers, leaving naught but bones.

I moved my paws from his shoulders and my rump from his pelvis. No need to hold him down any longer.

One task was accomplished, but I had more questions than answers.

"He's gone. Hurry," Aidyrth trumpeted from the sky not bothering with mind speech.

"Five minutes," I promised, raced to where I'd left my clothes, and reclaimed my human form.

This time, I found James in his bedchamber surrounded by a bevy of tits and asses in so many positions I had to count appendages to come up with four women. I swear, if he spent less time fucking and more time ruling, Scotland would be a better place.

He didn't notice me, so I pushed close to the bed. "Sire!" My tone was sharp.

He rolled out from beneath the entertainment committee, hissing and sputtering. "That's twice today. This better be good."

I eyed his scrawny chest and pathetic dick. My little finger is bigger. "I have news. Would you prefer it privately?"

He seemed to remember himself and shooed the women away.

"I'll be quick," I told him. "The deed you requested is done, but he carried poison. Nightshade from the smell of it. I tried to interrogate him, but he was too far gone. Make damn good and sure your royal tasters sample every single item at least an hour before you eat it."

For once, his dim little brain registered he might be in actual danger. Before he came up with something else for me to do, I said, "I'll be leaving for a few days. There are matters I must attend to elsewhere. When I return, I shall take possession of Inverness Castle."

"But I haven't actually discussed it with—"

"I don't care," I cut in. It was rude, but James was wearing on my nerves. I'd just carried out his latest assignment and warned him about a potential poisoning attempt. I knew him well enough not to expect gratitude, but there'd be hell to pay if he didn't honor his commitment to me.

"You must wait until—" He tried again but didn't get far.

"I'm moving there once I return," I spoke over him—again. "If anyone is still in residence, I'll make them very sorry."

"Now see here," he sputtered. "You work for me."

I rounded on him. "I do your bidding because the work pleases me. I am the one person in your court you can trust with your life. Do not even consider crossing me."

He shrank back against the bedclothes. Calling for his personal retinue was pointless. I terrified them.

Softening my tone, I said, "We have an understanding. I will see you upon my return."

"Where are you going?"

"Not your affair." Turning on my heel, I strode from his bedchamber nearly knocking down one of the women who'd had her ear glued to the door. I slapped her bare butt. "Hustle back in there," I suggested. "His highness could use a diversion."

She lingered, brushing naked flesh against my side. "And you, my lord?"

I laughed. "Find me once I return."

Aidyrth was scribing circles in the darkening skies when I burst into the courtyard. Before she could chide me for taking longer than five minutes, I executed a magic-assisted leap and landed squarely on her back.

Scotland's landscape turned dark as we entered a journey spell. Questions sat in the back of my throat. I didn't ask a one. Once we got to Cornwall would be time enough to glean details about what we faced.

"Thank you for allowing me latitude to complete my assignment," I murmured.

"Delilah is still alive," she replied.

"And she'll stay that way until we can extricate her."

I projected confidence and hoped to all the gods it was justified. The dragon would, indeed, burn down the world if anything happened to her bondmate. It wouldn't be pretty, and she was liable to blame me, the werewolf who'd placed killing a vampire over rescuing Delilah.

C ornwall's rocky coast was illuminated by moonlight
filtering through cloud cover. Tintagel, the castle
King Arthur had made famous, clung tenaciously to
rocks with a precipitous drop into the angry sea. Rain
pounded from the dark skies. Where it met the sea, it hissed
and bubbled.

"Delilah's been busy," I muttered.

"Furious is more like it," Aidyrth countered. "She
commands all forms of water. The sea and skies weep for her
predicament."

"How did this happen? Why were the two of you even in
Cornwall?" It was past time for me to know precise details
about Delilah's capture.

The dragon scudded into the surf and landed. I peered up
at a four-meter cliff slick with salt spray and barnacles. We
were protected from view here, but our next move eluded me.

"Delilah was an accomplished mage long before she and I met," Aidyrth explained.

"I knew as much."

Steam hissed from her open jaws. "Are you going to listen or not?"

"Tell me. I won't say another word until you're done."

"Better. The duke of Cornwall was an old friend of hers. He invited her to a gala celebrating his daughter's engagement."

Interesting. Unless I'd missed something, the duke's daughter couldn't be more than nine or ten, but early arranged marriages were common among royalty.

"We arrived a few days ago. At first, nothing appeared amiss. I remained in the background, a good choice as events unfolded. The second evening, guests collapsed where they sat. Over a score. I wouldn't have known, but my bondmate reached me telepathically.

"I ordered her to leave immediately, but she had other ideas. The duke was distraught. He needed her magic, and ten other excuses. I flew to a handy balcony and forced my way through into the ballroom."

"Bet that was well received," I mumbled.

"You said you'd hold your tongue."

"So I did. Sorry."

Fire streamed from her jaws, breaching the downpour. Steam hissed around us. "It was chaos. Pure chaos. Yelling and screaming. Guards and courtiers running this way and that. The reek of poison nearly undid me, and I have a strong stomach.

"The duke was screeching orders. No one paid him the slightest heed. I grabbed him in my forelegs and demanded to know what manner of deviltry reigned in his court."

"Bet he had no idea," I mumbled. Aidyrth had ordered me to listen, but remaining silent wasn't working.

"He did not. By then, the only mage left in the room was Delilah. She ran to me and pointed at the doors I'd ripped off their hinges.

"Go after them. They can't have gotten far."

"I asked who I was hunting. She explained three demonspawn had been masquerading as royalty from London.

"Missing the mark, as usual, the duke demanded names. We both ignored him."

The dragon shook herself from head to toe. Water droplets bounced off her scales. "By the time I returned—not having caught a single demon—Delilah was nowhere to be found. I grabbed the duke again, bound him with a truth spell, and forced him to speak."

I girded myself. Dragons can take days to come to the point. That Aidyrth had pared her recitation to a span of mere minutes bore testimony to how worried she was.

"The duke admitted to appointing a spate of assassins to rid him of a few troublesome nobles. He assumed the gala would provide the perfect cover. But he'd expected his hired killers would be circumspect. The last thing he imagined was the targets pitching facedown into their plates in clear view of the other guests."

"That's what you get for hiring demons," I muttered.

"Except he had no idea," Aidyrth pointed out.

"Doesn't make it any better. I'm still not clear how Delilah ended up in the dungeons and why she hasn't been able to extricate herself."

"The reason I couldn't find the demons is they're with Delilah, and she's not exactly in Cornwall's dungeon, but in a space between it and Hell."

"We can manage three demons. What are we waiting for?"

"I can't get to her. I tried before I hunted you down."

Aha. Always a glitch. "Is the barrier magical or physical?"

"Both. Do you require assistance?"

"Not sure. Give me a few minutes." I glanced up again and dropped my clothes on a handy rock. Once I'd secured them against the incessant wind, I shifted and made short work of the cliff.

As I'd expected, a sea door loomed. Unfortunately, it was inlaid with rusty iron grating. I called the dragon. Moments later, she hovered next to me, wings spread to take advantage of the wind.

I jerked my paw at the grating.

"Stand aside," she roared.

I barely had time to flatten myself against the vertical rocks when she cleaved a path through the bars with fire. They clattered against one another as they fell. The resultant opening was large enough to accommodate me, but not her.

Ducking inside, I found a surprisingly dry cavern perhaps ten meters across. Waves didn't reach this high, and the rain barely penetrated. My nostrils twitched seeking sulfur, ozone, and rot.

No demons anywhere near.

If I'd been in my mortal body, I'd have required a mage light, but my wolf's vision is sharp in dimly lit places. Padding forward, I crossed the cave and walked through a low, rounded archway. The stonework was surprisingly sophisticated. Someone who knew what they were about had created this escape route.

All of these old castles had secret corridors, ways noblemen could flee if the tide turned against them. If I looked hard, I bet I'd find a rope ladder affair tucked away to make scaling the cliff less dangerous.

The passageway twisted and turned. Soon, I came across a side path that had to lead to the castle dungeons judging from the smell.

Taking a chance, I raised my mind voice and called for Delilah.

No answer.

"Did you find her yet?" Aidyrth's voice pounded through my mind.

"Patience. I just got here."

"Hurry. Something doesn't feel right."

No more choice points after the channel leading to the dungeons. Made my life simpler. The path twisted this way and that, leading lower. If Aidyrth was right about Delilah's location I'd be there soon.

A rock clattered to the ground about a meter in front of me. Innocuous enough, I paid it no heed. Suddenly, I was in the midst of a meteor shower. That first rock had been a harbinger, not innocent at all. I sheltered beneath an overhang. Rocks found me anyway.

I tossed a ward together. It bought me time. The passageway was rapidly filling with rockfall. Speed was my friend. Stealth had just flown out the window. Someone knew I was here and was determined to pin me down.

Or force me to turn around. I was at the nexus where magical and physical barriers met.

No matter how I sliced and diced things, if I didn't move now, I wouldn't be able to—in either direction.

No contest. Not really. I released my mostly useless ward and slithered through the rapidly shrinking space above the rock pile. My paws took direct hits. Pain shot through my legs; I sent magic to knit the small bones back together.

I'd just pushed through a space that barely accommodated me when the clank of stone against stone told me my exit route was dead on arrival.

That exit route. I could teleport out of this shithole. And I wasn't leaving without Delilah.

Not sure what possessed me, I shouted her name. Words are terribly garbled in my werewolf form, but it's never stopped me. If she heard, she'd know it was me.

"Grigori!" floated back.

I tried to get a bead on what direction her voice had come from, but it echoed off the rocks, bouncing this way and that.

No matter. Pushing rocks out of my way, I clambered up, over, down, and up again. Blood flowed from dozens of cut places. I'm usually not sloppy. Leaving my blood fell into that category, but if I'd taken time to obliterate it, the tunnel would have closed. As it was, the spot a boulder had sealed the passage was only the first place. A dozen others rode in on its heels.

My weight atop the latest stack of rocks launched an avalanche. I clambered from rock to rock to stay on top of the tumbling mass. The tunnel must have come to an end. If the king of Hell placed conveniences like ladders, they'd been obliterated.

Rocks plummeted beneath me; others zinged past from above.

I had to remain on top of this mess, or I'd be buried the moment it hit bottom. And there had to be a bottom; even tunnels that bisected worlds didn't go on forever.

Flight isn't one of my magics. Too bad. Wings would have been a boon. Perhaps. Rockfall could have broken them. I switched from jumping on rocks below me to waiting for large ones to fall. When I spied a likely candidate, I leapt and waited for the next. My breath came fast, rasping from a throat dry from inhaling dust.

At least I wasn't blowing through magic. Nothing supernatural about this journey. I called Delilah's name again. This time, her response was much clearer.

"Say my name again," I urged. "Keep calling me."

The third time she screeched for me, I triangulated on her voice. Before our relative positions shifted, I cobbled a teleport spell together and ignited it. If she couldn't get out, maybe I wouldn't be able to breach the barrier around her, but I was sick of being battered by rocks.

Sooner or later, I'd have to punch my way through to her. May as well be before every bone in my paws had shattered. The noise and choking debris shimmered before finally fading to black.

I floated, the surcease from bounding from boulder to boulder more than a relief. Redirecting every shred of power at my disposal into my spell, I prepared to blast through anything standing between me and the water mage.

I've known Delilah longer than I've known the dragon. We were never lovers, but we have been good friends. Oftentimes, it's worth more since willing bedmates are common as goose grass.

I checked on my spell. Unless I was heading for a truly

remote sector of Hell, I should have arrived by now. Calling Delilah was no longer an option. She'd never hear me from within my teleport spell.

Naught to do but ride this out. I could switch destinations, but if I did, I'd blow my best—maybe my only—chance to rescue the water mage. And I'd incur the dragon's undying enmity.

Alienating her meant alienating every dragon. Not a pleasant prospect.

My paws ached. So did my chest. Probably cracked a rib during one of my aerial scrambles to keep from being crushed. The bleeding had stopped, but I'd left plenty to establish precisely who'd had the temerity to enter Satan's realm.

My spell finally, finally developed clear spots along its edges. I was about to arrive somewhere. Emerging from journey spells is a balancing act. I needed to maintain sufficient magic in the spell to see it through to its conclusion, but I also had to craft a ward and marshal defensive power. Not much good to fall into the enemy's hands naked as a newborn wolf.

"Try harder." Delilah's voice was shockingly near and not in telepathy.

A hand shot through the murk surrounding me and grappled with my fur until it snagged a handful of guard hairs and pulled hard. It hurt, but it also gave me what I needed to defeat the enchantment keeping us apart.

I fell through, knocking Delilah off her feet. "You always did have a flair for drama," she wheezed. Crawling out from under me, she stood and dusted herself off.

She never changes. Medium height with lush pale-blonde

curls that fell to her knees, she was a knockout. Gamine features and turquoise eyes with long lashes made her look about fifteen, even thought she was closing on several hundred years old. Her usual leather trousers were ripped in several places as was her trademark woolen tunic. The soft curves of her body always stole my breath.

"Nice work, Grigori," she growled. "What took you so long?"

I barked laughter. "Guess the thank-yous can come later."

"We're not out of here yet." She stated the obvious.

I shook myself from nose to tail tip, treading gingerly on my sore paws. "I got in. How come you couldn't get out?"

She spread her arms to highlight the small square room. "Do you see any water?" she demanded. "Even a trickle I could bend to my bidding?"

"Not here, but you did a fine job riling up the sea and the clouds."

"Fat lot of good it did me here," she retorted. "The water tried but failed to come within ten leagues of this spot."

"Where are we, exactly?" No doors led into this place. I hadn't expected any windows.

"Mmph. Best I can tell, a couple of steps removed from Hell proper."

"What does that mean?"

"None of the normal ways out work."

Naturally, she would have tried everything within the scope of her magic.

"Any idea why they singled you out?"

"I fell into the collateral damage category. When the demons' assassinations turned into a carnival sideshow, I was the only one who understood what had gone wrong. The demons knew they'd be outed for what they were. Before I could reveal them, they whisked me here."

She paused to take a breath. "Of course, they didn't count on my bond with Aidyrth. Or that I'd tell her everything."

"Perhaps they do know about the dragon," I suggested. "They placed you where she couldn't bail you out."

"Coincidence." She flapped a hand my way.

"Don't believe in them, but it's not relevant. We need to teleport out of here before your jailers pop in to check on you."

"They already did and left with their tails between their legs."

"What'd you do to them?"

"Better if you don't know."

The peculiar reek of hell deepened. I whirled, rising on my haunches in time to see a pair of richly dressed mages sashay through a black, fire-rimmed portal.

"Oh look," one said to the other. "We netted another one."

"Even better." The sorcerer rubbed long-nailed hands together. "It's a werewolf."

These weren't demons. No horns, hoofs, or tails. Meant they had to be dark princes. I've run across Michael and Beelzebub before. These two weren't them. Roughly my height—when I was in mortal form—they had broad shoulders and bare chests pierced with many copper rings. Black brocade robes sashed in red fell to ankle level. One had rust-colored curls. The other's hair was white and hung to the middle of his back. Two sets of black eyes with blood-red pupils examined me.

I stared back.

I love it when enemies forget to bind up their hair. It makes an attractive target.

"What do you want with my friend?" I growled, careful not to speak her name. They didn't need any more power over either of us.

"She will provide...entertainment." The white-haired one leered.

Delilah pranced next to me. "Like I entertained the demons who showed up here?"

"They were stupid," the redhead hissed.

Jagged blue darts flew from her fingertips, burying themselves in two crotches. "Does this make you stupid too?" she simpered.

Grunting in pain, the white-haired mage launched himself at Delilah. She was ready for him, but so was I. He grabbed and batted but couldn't penetrate the ward she'd tossed around herself.

While he was busy, I arced through the air, ignoring the pain in my feet, and closed my jaws around the side of his neck taking care to puncture the large vessels. The air filled with stinking black blood. I retched but didn't let go. For good measure, I wrapped a paw in his hair to make certain he couldn't escape.

Delilah had the other dark mage pinned on his back. Neat trick since she wasn't touching him, just standing over him. Daggers had materialized in either hand. Every time he moved, she slashed downward. Blue waves shimmered around her, turning the air hazy.

My target had gone down on both knees. He was losing too much blood to replenish it via any means. Any magic—

even the dark variety—required strength. Once a goodly portion of your blood is gone, you're not robust anymore.

Pinging and thunking drew my attention. Delilah had tacked the sorcerer neatly to the floor with a series of magical daggers. No matter how he twisted and writhed, they held him in place.

My guy gurgled through what was left of his windpipe, his blood filled with air bubbles. It was safe to leave him to his misery. He'd recover, but not for many days.

"We should leave," I barked.

"If the goddess wills it." Her tone was unexpectedly formal. She was worried, but she'd die before admitting it. "Are you going to shift?" she added.

I shook my shaggy head. "I'm stronger this way."

"I hope you can pull this off because I sure can't," she mumbled.

I'd been considering what would give us our best chance. It was counterintuitive, but our enemy wouldn't be expecting us to head deeper into no-man's land.

Not wanting to be overheard, I padded to Delilah and parked my head beneath her hand. She's always been quick, and I felt her deft probing as she plumbed my mind for details. Her eyes widened; her full lips spread in a grin.

"Brilliant. You've always been creative."

"Why thank you. Shall we see if it works?"

"Hurry. Someone else is coming."

I didn't how she knew. The dregs of the spell I'd used to get here still clung to me. I stitched them into something viable, draped netting over Delilah, and breathed new life into my casting.

Unlike my effort to get here, this piece of enchantment

took off like a shot duck. We plummeted through fire, brimstone, and heat that had my tongue lolling as I panted.

If we got lucky, we'd pass through a bottom somewhere and arc up the other side. I had no idea if a gateway would present itself, but I'd never come across any world that only had one entry point.

There had to be a way out.

We'd find it and live to fight another day.

Eh, we'd live period, and for a good long time. Forever in my case. Delilah is long-lived but not immortal. Still, I did not plan for either of us to waste any more time as demon fodder.

"It's getting cooler," she gasped.

I hadn't noticed, probably because of my thick coat. "I'll take your word for it."

Visions of water whooshed through me. Oceans of the stuff to cool me and slake thirst that had become a constant aching companion.

"Do not slack off now." Delilah wrapped an arm around my neck. The coolness of her power poured into me; I soaked it up like nectar.

"Can you sense your bondmate?" I wheezed.

Some of her magic departed. I filled in the hole quickly, but I was running out of steam. We had to break through soon, or we were finished—at least for now.

"She says—" Delilah began.

Cracking and booming drowned her out. I gathered my flagging energy, prepared to fight our way out of whatever stood between us and freedom.

I didn't have to.

My travel channel blew up around us. When the debris

cleared, Delilah and I were astride Adyrith's broad back. Mage and dragon were cooing to one another in the dragon's tongue.

I shut my eyes, soaking in the chill night breeze riffling my fur.

We'd escaped. It was enough for now. I could sort out how it actually happened later.

"Drop me at the nearest stream," I croaked.

"You're coming home with us," Delilah announced.

"Not Fire Mountain," I protested.

"I haven't lived there in centuries," Aidyrth informed me. "To be invited into a dragon's home is an honor. You forget yourself, werewolf."

I shut my eyes, too weary to do anything beyond clinging to the dragon's back. I'd been dead wrong about having any magic left. I was down to bedrock, tapped out. By Fenrir's grace, my misstep hadn't cost us dearly.

When I woke, I lay on a muddy bank next to a babbling brook, confused as hell about where I was. I'd fallen asleep as a wolf, but that part of my dual nature had fled leaving bruised and battered flesh. It required far more magic to heal the wolf, which was why he'd left me to my misery. Every cell of my body ached or stung.

Maybe not every single one, but enough to make me wish for a flagon of hundred-proof whiskey.

A groan escaped my raw throat, followed by one more. Crap. I sounded pathetic. Good thing the wolf wasn't front and center. He'd have cuffed me.

"Finally up, sleepyhead? I was starting to think a wicked witch ensorcelled you to sleep for a hundred years." Silvery laughter belonged to Delilah.

The fresh, clean scent of her magic married with water in the brook. I rolled to a sit and dropped my head into my hands to ease my throbbing temples. Opening my eyes took far too much effort.

"Here." She tipped a flask into my mouth. Gagging and choking, I finally figured out how to swallow again. Something in the liquid was more than water. It soothed my hurt places and eased the torment my body had become.

Peeling my lids open, I peered at her and rasped, "How come you're looking so chipper?"

She grinned. "I spent the last several hours in the sea."

"Pfft. Too bad I don't have something like that."

"You do. Here."

I took the flask from her and drained it.

"Feel like a rinse off? You still smell like demons." Her tone was far too cheerful.

I crinkled my nose, but I must have adapted to the stench. When I took stock of my body, I was naked. And then I recalled leaving my garments at the bottom of the sea wall.

Not a problem. Plenty more where they'd come from.

"Well?" Delilah pointed at the creek.

"What? No scented hot water with rose petals floating in it?"

"You're funny. How about you clean up. I'll gather the clothes Aidyrth rescued."

Thoughtful of the dragon. I'd always assumed they believed such conventions absurd.

Delilah had traded her leather pants and tunic for a violet silk robe embroidered with various sea creatures. It flapped around her legs as she started toward a stone castle perched on a nearby hilltop. Crafted of large irregular blocks held in place with mortar, rough-hewn timbers, and wavy glass, it blended nicely with the unruly landscape.

If I had to guess, we were somewhere in Northern Ireland.

I opened my mouth to tease Delilah about leaving a naked man to fend for himself but changed my mind. As I eased down the bank and into a deep pool, I focused on cleaning myself with scoops of sand. All my cut places raised hell, but I was determined. Once my body was clean, I tilted my head and scrubbed my scalp. Bits of bone and flesh—demon debris —were tangled in my long, red hair.

I should chop it off—and maybe I would—but not today.

Feeling slightly more alive, I clambered up the bank and sat on a patch of grass. Weak rays from a pallid sun dried me. Dozing off again was tempting, but I had to get back to Edinburgh. James was a sly one. I could see him welching on a technicality.

Something like, "Well, you weren't here, so I figured you'd changed your mind about Inverness Castle."

The delightful zing of Delilah's magic announced her arrival.

"Here you go." She plopped an armload of clothes next to me and sat beside them.

"I must be losing my touch," I joked.

She screwed her face into a question mark. "Whatever do you mean?"

"Most women wouldn't hustle off while I was naked."

The question mark shaded to a soft smile. "I came back, didn't I?"

I'd been teasing. Was she? In all the years I've known Delilah, we'd never so much as exchanged a kiss. We'd shared blood and guts and gore, but never passion.

"Aidyrth wants to talk with you," she said and patted my stack of garments. "Much as I'm enjoying the scenery, it's best not to keep her waiting."

I scooped my clothes up, moved them to my other side, and scooted next to Delilah. She didn't protest when I put an arm around her. Before I could turn her head, she did it for me and kissed me, her mouth pliant and full of promise.

I threaded fingers through her luxuriant fair locks and held her head in place while I teased the inside of her mouth with my tongue. Her breath quickened; she wrapped her arms around me. The press of hardening nipples against my chest sent waves of heat spilling through me.

My nether region came alive with need.

"I said now," thundered through Delilah's head loud enough for me to hear.

She dragged her mouth from mine. "Inconvenient, but duty calls."

I didn't see why I had to march to the dragon's beat, but she had rescued us. It placed me firmly in her debt. Bypassing her summons was rude and might mean I'd end up on her "bad mage" list—if dragons kept such things.

Not an appealing prospect.

Delilah was handing me clothes. Before I pulled my trousers all the way up, she ran an index finger up my shaft. "Hold onto that pose, tiger."

"It's wolf." I laughed and hustled into the rest of my garments.

Leaning into each other, we walked up the hill to the castle. The dragon met us in the courtyard. I bowed. "Thank you for salvaging my clothing and for your assistance extricating us from, well from wherever we were."

Aidyrth inclined her head. Scales clanked. "You located my bondmate. I am in your debt. Name what you would have from my hoard."

Surprise riffled through me. "It's fine. Really. I'm honored, but—"

"Choose something," she roared through a gout of flames.

"You must tell him the truth," Delilah spoke up.

I looked from mage to dragon and asked, "What truth?"

"'Tis binding," Aidyrth mumbled.

Binding, eh. "In what way?"

"Not as she and I are bound," Delilah explained. "Still, if she has need of you, you will be compelled to obey."

I bowed even lower. My mind brimmed with ways to avoid offending the dragon while still maintaining my independence. "If you have need of me, rest assured I will come. I answer to no one unless I choose it, but I have been thinking about the assassin trade lately."

"What does that have to do with my offer?" Smoke and ash followed her words.

"Nothing directly." I inhaled cautiously. "Before my last job for James, I requested Inverness Castle as payment. At the time, I had no idea what I'd do with a castle, but it's becoming clearer."

"What's becoming clearer. You're talking in riddles," Delilah said.

"Probably because this idea is brand new. It began taking shape while I cleaned demon scum off myself in the creek."

"Water has a way of clarifying things." She sounded pleased her element had accepted me. Or maybe smug. It was hard to tell.

Even though my thoughts remained scattered, I dove in.

Delilah and Aidyrth were my friends. They'd forgive a half-baked aspect to my recitation.

"The assassin trade has fallen on hard times lately," I began.

"What do you mean?" Aidyrth trumpeted impatiently. "I'm as efficient as ever. So is Delilah."

"You are." I nodded. "But many noblemen are hiring inept tradespeople. Because kings, princes, and the rest of their ilk aren't sensitive to power, they sometimes hire demons or other sorcerers—rather like the duke of Cornwall did."

"Pfft." More fire. "It's always been a problem."

It's dangerous to contradict dragons, but in this case, it was necessary. "Sorry, but the problem has grown worse. In the past span of days, I've been called on to intervene in two messes that could have been avoided if our business had standards."

"And how are you planning to accomplish that?" Aidyrth snapped her jaws impatiently.

"The same way any trade does, by forming a guild."

There. It was out. I'd said it. I looked expectantly at my audience.

"A guild." Delilah cocked her head to one side. "I rather like the idea."

Encouraged, I hurried on. "If it works as I hope, I will provide a central location for all assassination requests. They will run through me. I guarantee results and can match the assassin with the job. It could work. But there's one more element I'm toying with."

"Which is?" Aidyrth crossed her forelegs over her scaled chest.

"Every assassin in the guild will be bonded with an animal. Unless they're like me and hold a dual nature."

"This is getting better all the time." Delilah clapped me across the back.

"First, I have to clear out Inverness Castle to provide a home for mages in between jobs."

"Would we have to live there?" Aidyrth asked.

I took it as a good sign she was seriously considering the idea. "Of course not, but it would be there if needed. For mages and their bond animals to prep for jobs and recover afterward."

The more I talked about it, the more excited I became.

"Why stop at one guild house?" Aidyrth asked.

"Aye, the assassins I know live in many spots on this world and others," Delilah chimed in.

"There could be more than one as this project grows." I held up a cautionary hand. "Right now, I'm not even certain the idea will be attractive to the noblemen who'd have to trust me enough to turn delicate matters my way."

"There is that," Delilah mumbled.

"You could place them in a difficult position if you ever revealed who'd hired you to do what," the dragon added.

I shook my head. "I'm not going to bribe them to accept the guild concept. Kings have employed assassins to rid themselves of annoying presences in their courts since the dawn of time. That part isn't going to change."

"Aye, but they're used to dealing with their own personal assassins," Adyrith pointed out. "That will change since they'd be losing control over who carries out their wishes."

"Ergo the trust part," I inserted. "I have no idea if this is going to hold universal appeal, but if we don't do something, we're going to get a terrible reputation that will smear us all. No one will recognize the duke of Cornwall screwed himself by hiring demons. All they'll see is a botched poisoning.

"Speaking of which, I warned James to make certain his tasters check every scrap of his food."

"Will he?" Delilah asked.

I shrugged. "Depends on how hungry he is."

"It should depend on how badly he wants to live," the dragon rumbled along with more smoke.

"He's been king since he was not quite two years old. It's convinced him he's untouchable. James isn't the issue here," I clarified. "I need to reach out to the assassins I know to float the guild concept."

"How can we help?" Delilah asked.

"We could come up with a list. You approach some; I'll talk with others. Shouldn't take too long to determine if enough of us are interested."

"I can see the appeal," Delilah said. "Dealing with supernatural creatures adds a layer of protection. Not that we're easy to kill, but remember all the mortal assassins who've been hanged by irate kings."

I hadn't considered that aspect, but it was significant. I wasn't especially fond of dealing with humans, either, but if I kept it strictly business—maybe conducted affairs through a courier sworn to maintain my anonymity—it would reduce the unpleasant part.

"I'd have to offer cheap rates at the front end," I murmured, thinking out loud.

"Why?" Aidyrth sounded flabbergasted.

Never tell a dragon there might be a decrease in their cut of anything.

"To prove how smoothly things can run. It's better if whoever hires the work has no idea about anything beyond the finished product. I'd collect half up front and half when the job is done, and—"

"Absolutely not," Aidyrth trumpeted. "All the funds up front. If they don't trust you enough to compensate you, you'll have hell to pay collecting."

"Eh, perhaps you're right." I sank into a crouch. "Clearly, this needs more thought."

"First let's see if any of us are interested," Delilah said firmly. "If we can't come up with an initial cadre, there's not much point in pouring more energy into it." She narrowed her eyes. "You're tired."

"Not as bad as when I woke, but aye. 'Twill be a while before I've recovered."

"Take him inside and feed him," Aidyrth instructed. "I'll do a bit of reconnaissance. By the time I've returned we'll know more."

Before I could thank her for her faith in me, she spread her reddish wings and was gone.

"I haven't seen her that interested in anything in years," Delilah commented and dragged me upright.

"I could go home," I said.

"Why would you want to? I'm here. Besides, Aidyrth will expect an audience upon her return."

There were worse places to be—lots worse. I was still concerned about James's promise of Inverness Castel, but if he tried to welch, I'd make him exceedingly sorry. So sorry, he'd pull out every kingly trick to make things right.

Like all effective assassins, I had the goods on him. Pithy

little bits that could do untold damage if they saw the light of day.

Delilah tugged on my arm. "Come inside before you fall down."

I laughed. "Yes, darling. You have my undivided attention."

She shook a finger under my nose. "I'd better. You don't want to know what happened to the last man who crossed me."

"You already said that. I bet you stuffed demon balls down demon throats."

"That and worse. Hell can't compete with an aggravated water mage."

I laced my fingers with hers. "Anyone who doesn't recognize it is stupid."

From the courtyard, we walked up a grassy hill and stone steps. Once we reached the front doors, she twisted to face me and crushed her mouth over mine.

I hadn't imagined her interest. Flattered and hotter than the hell we'd narrowly escaped from, I returned her kiss with everything left in me.

5

My exhaustion vanished, blown away in the face of sexual heat. Mostly, I've lusted after mortals. Mages live far too long, and the odds of maintaining a love interest over centuries don't stack up well.

Not that I was thinking about anything other than the lithe magic of the woman in my arms. The "why me" and "why now" questions could wait. Maybe forever.

She ran her mouth down my neck, her tongue leaving a hot trail across my skin. I trailed my hands the length of her spine and cupped the globes of her ass, drawing her hips against me.

Cushioned by her belly, my errant member swelled to fullness. In a distant part of my mind, my wolf howled with delight. If it were up to him, we'd have sex several times a day rather than on my schedule, which wasn't often. Most women need wooing, and I never had free time to devote to the project.

Delilah cradled the back of my neck with one hand. She jammed the other between us and cupped it around my shaft. Something suspiciously like a purr teased my ears.

I backed us up against a stone wall and captured her mouth with mine again. Her breath was hot and sweet. The salt smell of the sea wafted around us, enticing and soothing at the same time. Little nipping bites traded with suckles and licks.

Wanting her was all-consuming. "Sure you're not part Siren?" I teased when my mouth wasn't busy with hers.

Eyes that had darkened to midnight blue latched onto my gaze. "You have it mixed up, wolfman. I came first. They're but a pale imitation."

A spear of worry intruded, but I was too entranced to pay it any heed. This was Delilah, not some arcane sorceress out to steal my free will with seduction.

The front of her robe fell open—or maybe she pushed it out of the way. Her breasts were perfect, works of art. Men would have fought battles over those breasts. High, full, perfect. Tipped with copper-colored nipples the size of gold doubloons, they deserved kissing, adoration.

Bending my head, I nipped and bit first one and then the other. She moaned, leaning into me. Her nipples lengthened and grew harder, encouraging me to heights of inventiveness. She'd moved sideways and straddled one of my legs. Heat from her core sent jets of lust up my leg where she rubbed her sex against it.

She still had hold of me and was rubbing my member lazily, teasing it with each stroke.

We hadn't moved out of the castle doorway, but I didn't care. We could have been anywhere. How could I have missed what a gem she was? We'd worked together on dozens of assassinations. And gone our separate ways afterward.

The salt smell of the sea thickened around us; the castle dissolved into mist leaving us on a lush tropical shore. She pushed me onto warm sand beneath a stand of some kind of palm tree, except these had pink fronds and a hibiscus-like scent.

The laces holding my trousers together had come undone. I hadn't touched them, so she must have. She tossed a leg over me and sat on my thighs. Her robe had been shoved back displaying arched ribs, a slender waist, flared hips, and a mass of fair curls protecting her sex.

I settled my hands on her hips intent on moving her over my shaft. She was so close, the musk of her tantalized me, blending with the sea smells around us. Breakers crashed on the beach. Gulls cawed overhead.

When she resisted my invitation, I pinched and tugged at her nipples and ran my fingertips over silken skin.

"I like your idea," she murmured.

My brain was so saturated with lust, all roads pointed to sex. I dropped my hands to her hips once again. "Then crawl on. We're both ready."

"Not that idea, silly."

"Which one, then?" I was drawing a blank.

"The group of assassins. Imbuing our trade with standards." She wrapped her fingers around me again, squeezing lightly. Sensation spilled through me that had nothing to do with my brainchild. That brain had taken a distant backseat to the other one.

"We can talk about it later," I murmured, still intent on the heat of her surrounding me.

She nodded. "That too. For now, I would rule with you. Aidyrth likes the idea. She is willing to be your dragon advisor."

Alarm bells blared, jolting me back to reality. In an unceremonious gesture, I upended her as I got my feet under me. "So that's what this was about," I sputtered, lust turning to ashes.

She scrambled to her feet. "Not entirely. I've always liked you, Grigori."

"I like you too"—I blew out a tired breath—"or I did before you tried to manipulate me." Making a grab for my pants, I pulled them up and secured the laces.

"That's harsh." She placed a hand on my arm.

I brushed it off and faced her. "Living a long time has advantages. One is I know myself well enough to understand I don't have the personality to share power— with anyone."

Plowing on, I added, "If this project grows wings, I must have absolute control over it. We will engage in group decision making, but if there are disagreements, I will have the final word."

"So that's how it is?" She placed both hands on her hips. Her robe still stood open, but I averted my gaze. Staring at the merchandise, knowing it wasn't for me, would only make me miserable.

"That's how it is. I'd have liked it better if you'd been honest about your intentions rather than using seduction to lure me to your point of view."

"Be fair," she pouted.

"I call things as I see them."

Not much reason to remain here any longer. With passion

receding, my earlier exhaustion had returned. I had plenty of magic to get back to Scotland, or I thought I did.

Depended on where she'd taken us.

As I conjured a teleport spell to take me to Edinburgh, I pushed my annoyance aside and bowed slightly. "I hope you and your bondmate will still be interested in being part of my project. None of the reasons for formalizing our trade have gone away.

"If someone doesn't pick up the reins, it leaves the door wide open for slipshod assassination attempts and dark mages to swoop in and take advantage of the confusion."

She pressed her delicious lips together. "My offer is still open."

"Mine is not related to yours." Breath swooshed from me. "I'd welcome you into my bed, Delilah, but not on a quid pro quo basis. Either you want me for me, or I'm not interested."

Her lips formed a pout. "Why can't I have both?"

It was a child's question, and it made me smile. "Because life doesn't work like that. We rarely get all of what we hope for."

"I have a pretty good track record."

"Ha. I just bet you do." On that parting note, I ignited my spell.

It took longer than I expected before my humble room under the eaves of Edinburgh castle took shape. I really should hunt down James. Instead, I pitched onto my narrow pallet and shut my eyes. Beneath me, my cock still throbbed with unslaked lust.

Damn Delilah to Hell and back.

Nay, damn me for falling for the oldest trick in a woman's playbook. Or almost falling for it. Lucky for me, she'd hit on a sore spot. I've tried being part of group projects; unless there's a clear leader, they never go well.

Assassins are a headstrong bunch, used to working independently. If I was going to instill order, I'd have to start with a firm hand and hang onto it. Tough to do if a partner counseled a different path.

I'd make plenty of mistakes, but fixing them would be relatively simple, not requiring lengthy discussions—or consensus.

I'd done the right thing. For me and my yet-to-be-formed guild.

Drifting, half conscious, half not, visions of bouncing breasts and slick pussies ebbed and flowed. Release took me with almost no effort. In my fantasy, my partner had coal black hair and rode a unicorn. It wasn't until later I recognized her. Or thought I did. It's not as if I've ever seen her body.

Rhiana is another mage, this time of the elemental variety. She and her unicorn, Dorcha, have been bonded for centuries. Elemental mages are ancient, and unlike Delilah, who controls a single element, they control all four.

I hadn't exactly slept, but then I rarely do. After a rinse off in a large clawfoot tub, I donned fancier garments. A cream silk shirt and black woolen pants. James was quite the dandy, and he appreciated quality clothing. Boots and a bronze torc around my neck completed my outfit.

It was closing on suppertime. I expected to find my regent at least tipsy as he prepared for the dinner hour. He didn't disappoint me. Lounging in his usual dining area, he was surrounded by tasters.

At least he'd taken my worries about poisoning seriously.

He reached for a plate of quail's eggs, only to have the taster in charge of that plate step between James and the food. "Not yet, Regent. Another quarter hour must pass."

James shut his eyes, muttered, "This is ridiculous," and slumped in his throne chair. When he opened his eyes and scanned the room, he saw me and pointed. "All your fault," he grumbled.

I hurried forward but stopped shy of bowing or scraping or kissing his ass. "If you're referring to waiting to eat, have any of your tasters met with problems?"

"Aye, but they recovered."

He couldn't very well gloss over reality in a roomful of men offering up their lives to protect his.

"Not such a bad idea, then." I aimed for a light note.

The quail egg taster made a retching noise and turned away. Others held a bucket for him to vomit into. He started out of the chamber but fell to his knees.

Oh-oh. Judging from his gray face, this might not end well.

Healing isn't my first magic, but mortals are pretty simple creatures. I ran to his side and knelt, probing with magic to determine the problem. He was bleeding internally. Another few minutes, and he'd be beyond anyone's help.

The other men had withdrawn to a respectful distance, or maybe a terrified one. Magic makes mortals uncomfortable. They might leave offerings, but mostly to ensure nothing amiss befalls them.

James had gotten up off his ass. He stood over us. "What's wrong with him?"

"Ask me later."

It was rude, especially to a king, but I was busy.

Normally, I'd have asked permission from the stricken

man, but he'd passed out. Reaching deep within him, I patched the torn vessels, and then moved on to damaged organs. I took my time, making certain not to miss anything. When I'd averted the crisis, I brewed an antidote from materials I'd requested, tilted his head, and dribbled it down his throat. He swallowed reflexively.

"He'll live," I told his fellows. "Take him to his bed. Make certain he drinks a lot of water and spends time out of doors for a few days."

Amid many thank-yous, several courtiers rolled the still unconscious man onto a pallet and carried him out of the room.

"Leave us." James motioned to those still left in the room. They shuffled out without a word. My healing had no doubt unnerved them.

After putting stoppers into beakers and gathering my mess into one spot, I stood and stared at James. "You were saying about the inconvenience of tasters?"

"Never mind," he mumbled.

I dropped a hand onto his shoulder. He flinched but didn't order me not to touch him. "You need to assign someone to figure out where those quail eggs came from," I told him. "Do it immediately while the trail is still warm. Once you determine who's out to get you, I'll end them, and you can dispense with others eating your food first."

He yelled for the head of his guardsmen.

Before the man showed up, I said, "Inverness Castle? I am planning to take possession immediately."

He snarled. "Oh that."

"Aye. You promised."

"Did I now?"

Nice wasn't working very well. I tightened my grip on his shoulder. "You. Do. Not. Want. To. Cross. Me. You know full well what I'm capable of."

He blinked owlishly. "You wouldn't dare."

"Watch me. If it weren't for me, you'd be dead."

"You can't know that." His tone was petulant.

I jerked a thumb in the direction of the door the fallen man had exited through. "Aye, but I can. And do. If it weren't for my edict about tasters, you'd have eaten those eggs. I might not have been here—"

"Our healers could have taken care of the problem," he pronounced.

I laughed, long and loud. "If you believe that, you have a bigger problem than I imagined. Besides"—I lowered my voice—"the harsh truth is your people do not like you. No one would go out of their way to pull you back from death's door."

His mouth opened and shut like a fish on a hook. No one ever spoke plainly to him. It wasn't part of his experience.

"Back to Inverness Castle," I continued. "I will travel there tomorrow. If anyone is still in residence, I will ensure they depart swiftly."

"But I need at least a week," James protested.

I narrowed my eyes. "What will you do with that week?"

"Why evict them. What else?"

Finally, he'd come around to honoring his promise to me. I waited through a space of a few minutes to let him know I was considering his offer, but it was far from a done deal.

"You have one week from today," I said at last. "Not an hour more."

This time, I slipped a dirk from the ankle sheath where I usually carry it and grabbed James's right hand.

"What are you doing?" he screeched and tried to yank away from my grip.

"Making certain you make good on your word."

"Unhand us this instant. It's wholly unnecessary," he sputtered.

"I believe it is."

I sliced a short cut in the ball of his thumb and then one in mine. Still holding tight, I rubbed the cut places together while he struggled to get away.

"Will I turn into...into something like you?" His tone shrilled with terror.

"You should be so lucky. Nay, nothing that eventful will befall you. But if you welch on our deal, you will suffer the torments of the damned."

It wasn't exactly true, but he had no way of knowing. His already pasty complexion turned even whiter.

Bending, I gathered the items I'd used to heal the quail egg eater and strode casually from the room.

6

Between wimpy kings and power-mad bitches, I needed a break. Rather than returning to my room, I left the castle and loped toward nearby hills. Somewhere along the way, I shucked my garments and captured my wolf form, not caring who saw me shift.

We ran and ran, glorying in the simple joy of movement. Herds of sheep and goats raced in the opposite direction. They had naught to fear from me. I hunted in this body, but never so close to home.

While I ran, I fleshed out my ideas. Assassins are independent operators. For them to join a like-minded group required more than persuasion. I'd have to prove it would be worthwhile for them.

One of the biggest advantages was they'd be one step removed from arbitrary monarchs, who insisted on interfering in every aspect of the operation. James wasn't like that, but I'd accepted jobs where the regent in question demanded to be present while I worked. Since many of them were either squeamish or shockingly bloodthirsty, they'd often gotten in my way.

Assassins are most effective when we're invisible. Having an unwelcome sidekick had come back to bite me more than once. The monarch never got into lasting trouble, mostly because they disavowed all knowledge and blamed me. But I'd ended up with a lynch-hungry mob on my heels. It wasn't accidental that every assassin I knew was some sort of mage.

Mortals had decided the trade was far too dangerous. Simpler to kill on their terms rather than being someone's murder-for-hire shill.

Why did I stick it out?

I've asked myself that question many times. What I always come up with is I enjoy being at the center of political intrigue. I need a reason to kill, but I'm discriminating. I reserve the right to say no if the assignment doesn't appeal to me.

For example, if the target hasn't done anything more serious than ruffle a few feathers, I won't be part of their downfall. So many kings and princes hold ridiculously inflated views of themselves. It's good for them to run into the odd person who reflects reality.

Still sorting how to proceed, I ran for a long while. Heart pounding, tongue lolling, I flopped onto a rock. The sun, a rare enough occurrence, kissed my fur.

The more I considered my idea, the better I liked it. I'd set up a central point of contact. Assignments would flow through me. When mages weren't working for me, they'd be free to pursue whatever so long as it didn't reflect unfavorably on my little group. The inclusion of bond animals would keep everything on the up and up. They have principles and are loyal to a fault. Another plus is their senses are far more finely honed; it alerts them to subtle cues.

Magic can do much the same—if it's deployed. But maintaining such a spell blows through scads of enchantment. Far simpler to have an animal partner taking care of that part of things.

All mages are capable of bonding with animals, magical or otherwise. Despite that, very few have bondmates, but it could change.

Actually, it had to change if my idea had a chance of bearing fruit.

Very few know this, but magical animals have their very own world. I'm only privy to part of it. Werewolves are one-of-a-kind. Contrary to urban myths, we're not formed because one of us bit a mortal. We've only hung onto that fable because it's simpler if humans are afraid of us.

And they give us a very wide berth.

With good reason. The only mortals I bite die because I've decided to end them.

My thoughts were wandering far afield. My kind originally came to be when a forest wolf happened upon a field of rotten grain. Something about the decay created airborne bits. When he inhaled them, they rendered him unconscious, but they also conferred our dual nature.

The many-times-over great grandfather of werewolves recognized he'd stumbled onto a miracle. After he'd transitioned forms a few times—to make certain the ability was real—he took to his wolf form and spread the word.

Soon every wolf in his pack and others nearby had staked a claim to were-status.

They hadn't counted on the church. Of course, they hadn't. They'd not spent any time as men, so they had no idea how superstitious and narrowminded mankind can be.

After losing several of their kin to traps, early werewolves grew more circumspect. They gathered a cache of the magical grain, hoarding it in a secret location. And they quit spreading the word about the miraculous substance that conferred our unique nature.

Mortals couldn't kill us, but they could make us miserable. Between salt and fire and holy water, being captured was worse than being dead.

A few of us discovered if we mated, we'd produce others just like us. By this time, I'd come into the picture, so I was part of the discussion that sealed up what was left of the grain for good. It wasn't as if the world required more werewolves. We live forever. Too many could pose a huge problem.

Magical animals are nothing like us. For one thing, they are what they are. No shapeshifting—unless they're slated to partner with a shapeshifting mage. In those cases, the mage flows into them to accomplish the shift. When he (or she) leaves, the animal still exists but on another plane.

The animals destined to bond with shapeshifting mages appear in dreams and visions. Mages already know their animals by the time they show up, usually when the mage enters sexual maturity.

By contrast, my wolf and I are the same. Two guises sharing a single physicality. When the man is in ascendance, the wolf resides within. For other shapeshifter duos, the animal retreats to their magical world when the mage is in human form.

At least, it's how I believe it works. None of us are truly conversant with magic beyond our own.

I've visited the animals' world before but never been allowed past the gatekeeper. Regardless, I needed to try once more. This was important—to me. We'd see how good a salesman I was pitching the bondmate idea to animals who had no need to alter their status quo.

The sun was sinking into the North Sea when I abandoned my rock. Figuring I might have better luck if I retained my wolf's body, I set a spell to take me to the animals' world.

I needed their cooperation for my plan to work. If an unbonded mage wanted to join my company of assassins, they'd need to partner up. I had no idea if the animals would be intrigued by such an arrangement. Or if they'd boot me out of their world with instructions never to return.

Journey spells hold a timeless quality. It could have been ten minutes or ten hours before the edges of my spell turned translucent moments before I reached a glowing gateway.

I stopped in front of the silvery arch and waited.

A zebra trotted through and stopped hoof to paw with me. "What brings you to our world, Grigori?"

She knew my name, but I had no idea who she was.

Hunkering on my belly to show I ceded dominance, I said, "I would very much appreciate an audience before your council."

The zebra brayed what might have been laughter. "Our what?" She choked out.

I swallowed annoyance and rose to my feet. I'd be damned if I'd demean myself for no reason.

"I have an idea. It would go more smoothly if I had cooperation from you."

"I'm listening." The zebra stamped a hoof.

"By you, I meant all the animals," I clarified.

"I speak for my people."

How could that be? Still, who was I to question their social structure.

"Are you certain you don't want to include others?" I asked, ignoring my internal instructions not to make unnecessary waves.

"I may choose to do so. Depends on what you want. You have a short time. Make use of it or leave."

Great. Meant I might have to tell my story several times.

So what if I do. This is important. If I can't make this part work, none of the rest will, either.

I shook myself from head to tail tip and hoped I didn't sound as put out as I felt when I said. "As you may know, I work as an assassin for several courts. Not at the same time, mind you, but I get around, and I take pride in my work. Over the years, I've noticed many problems.

"Some assassin work is sloppy. Others create more problems than they solve. My plan is to form a"—I searched for just the right word—"circle of assassins made up of mages bonded with animals."

So far, the zebra hadn't shut me up. Her ears were pricked forward, so she was at least listening.

"It will take a little doing," I continued, "but I plan to form a central point of contact for every court. If a monarch or regent requires assassin services, they will contact me, and I will toss it out to the circle to see who is best suited for the task."

"What's in it for these mages?" The zebra stared at me out of dark eyes.

"Simplicity. Anonymity. Getting out from under dealing with kings. Being part of an organization with high standards."

"I see. And what's in it for bond animals?"

"A fair question. Few mages choose to partner with magical animals, but many assassins have already formed bonds. There wouldn't be a huge increase. The circle shouldn't number more than fifty or so at full capacity, and it will take years to build it to that level."

She pawed the ground. "You didn't answer my question."

My upper lip wanted to curl, showing fang. I resisted the urge. "You're right. I didn't. Not directly." I shook myself again to buy thinking time. "I have no idea how things work in this world, or if there are animals who want to bond with mages but can't find appropriate partners.

"If there are even a few, this could solve their problem."

It was a decent place to stop, so I did.

"Would the animals have a choice?"

"Of course."

"How would it work? Would the mages show up here?"

I hadn't actually gotten that far, so I chucked the ball back her way. "How would you like it to work?"

She nodded. Perhaps my question pleased her. "The mages would have to present themselves here, so we could lay eyes on them. And then the animals would pick who will bond with a particular mage."

It sounded fair to me. The only sticky wicket was most mages would probably want to do the picking. Her suggestion might be a hard sell. Or not. I had no idea how excited mages would be at the prospect of a brand-new bond animal.

I angled my head. "Does this mean we have a deal?"

"Perhaps. Return in two days' time."

"Are you sure there's no one else for me to talk with about this?"

"Aye." Turning, she trotted back through the glowing arch. It winked out, leaving me teetering on the edge of a world about to discard me.

I resurrected my journey spell and left before things grew unpleasant. Because it made sense, my next stop had to be Inverness. I'd use the castle as my first base of operations. The circle would grow over time—if I could get if off the ground. For now, the castle would provide our first home.

I've lived so long, not much excites me.

This did. It had to mean I was on the right track.

I tweaked my spell to bring me out in dense woods north of the castle. While my wolf form had been perfect for my visit to the animals' world, now I needed to be human with clothing.

I could return to Edinburgh. Or I could resolve the garment issue in another way. It was early evening with many passersby. Remaining a wolf—or being naked—wouldn't serve my interests. Rich people had locking doors—and servants. The poor, not so much. Of course, they rarely had a change of clothing to spare.

As I considered what to do, I settled into my man's body. The fur on my hands and feet is always the last to go.

Lack of clothing left me with a dilemma. I didn't want to rob a peasant of his only set of breeks or his only tartan, so I crafted an invisibility spell, left the woods, and took to alleys hunting for manor houses with lines of drying laundry. It didn't take long to find what I sought.

A pinch of magic coupled with a don't-look-here spell netted me homespun breeks and a rough shirt. Perfect to fade out of anyone's memory. No one paid the slightest heed to unfortunates.

I'd just scrambled into my purloined finery when something made the skin on the backs of my hands crawl. Instinct told me to spin around, power raised against whoever felt so foul, but if I did I'd reveal myself.

Better to shamble away.

"I saw what you did," a hoarse voice hissed.

So much for slithering out of sight. At least I wasn't dealing with the king's guard. They'd have slapped me in irons for thievery.

The alley was deserted. Easy to dispatch whoever stood a few paces away. Summoning defensive magic until it crackled from my hands, I spun.

And stopped dead.

Vampires. At least six blocked my way.

Why hadn't I smelled them?

"Just look at the pretty werewolf," one sneered.

"Oh, you mean the pretty werewolf who killed one of our own?" Another grinned, displaying fangs.

Everything clicked into place. Word had gone out. Every vampire in the Highlands—except Logan and his seethe—was looking for me because of what I'd done to Lord Willoughby, though I doubted he actually was a lord.

Before this seedy batch got too comfy, I issued a bloodcurdling shriek and piled into them.

7

My shriek had been purposeful. Vampires were a scourge. If anyone came running, they'd take one look and leap into action to help me—ostensibly a poor peasant set upon by evil.

The vampires knew what I was, but no one would listen to them.

Long, dirty nails grazed my wrist. I pivoted out of the way and ran right into another of the abominations. Since they didn't need to lure me, their rotten blood stench was suddenly thick. Contrary to popular opinion, werewolves do not dine on carrion. My stomach balled into a hard knot.

Someone barreled into me from behind, driving me to the ground. Maybe two someones. They were strong. I twisted and turned desperate to escape fangs puncturing my neck.

Hot breath told me someone was close, too close for comfort.

I'd wanted to avoid magic in case my yelp had drawn someone's attention. Far better to appear helpless. Mortals don't trust magic, and a contest between a couple of iterations of sorcery wouldn't encourage anyone to jump to my defense.

Nope. If they suspected I batted for the other side, they'd leave me to rot before they'd help.

Weight bore down on me until my ribs creaked in protest. Pain shot up my spine. Teeth grazed my neck.

"What are you waiting for?" one shouted.

"Aye, send him to his doom," another encouraged.

"No immortality for him," another chimed in helpfully.

Fuck this.

They were toying with me, drawing out the torment. Maybe blood tastes better if the victim is scared half out of their mind.

I wasn't afraid, but I was furious.

I also had no idea what impact being bitten would have on me. If any werewolves have been vampire bait, it's not noted in the lore books.

For good reason.

The werewolf in question would have been too heartily ashamed to admit being captured.

Or maybe they turned into vampires, a smart-ass inner voice suggested. It would have shut them up too.

The crew standing around us began to chant, "Bite. Bite. Bite," like a demented cheering squad.

For fuck's sake.

I was beyond caring if help was on the way. After calling on earth magic to rise to my aid, I absorbed its energy through my belly.

And let it grow. The queasy knot from vampire stench retreated.

My enemies were oblivious. Their connection to the natural world ended the moment they drank their maker's blood.

I thrashed back and forth, aiming for a realistic demonstration of fear.

Soon, very soon, I'd have what I needed.

Like a thick, sweet syrup, earth power saturated every cell. Another moment, and I'd transform all that enchantment into enough strength to shake off the ones splayed on top of me.

Something hard pressed against the side of my neck. I was out of time. Any abrupt movement would impale me. The fang wasn't hovering over a major vessel, but close enough.

Their saliva has mesmerizing qualities; I needed every scrap of mental clarity to worm out of this mess. Being turned was not on the menu. Not today or ever.

A silver stake or two would help, but I was fresh out of those.

No salt or holy eater, either.

Grabbing hold of the swollen flow of earth magic, I directed it to the point in my neck directly below the vampire's fang and twisted beneath his touch. Given I couldn't see, I got lucky.

My aim ran true.

The shock of clean, pure power was too much for the vampire. He bellowed as if he'd been burned. Maybe he had. The opportunity I'd been waiting for swatted me across the shoulders.

I gathered surplus earth magic into a shield and punched

the vampires on my back as hard as I could. Amid grunts and bellows, I shoved them off me. The transition from flat on my stomach to leaping through the air would have done my wolf proud.

He yipped approval from where he lives within me and built a case for ascendency. Hard to argue his was the superior form for this contest, but I'd started this, and I'd be damned if I wouldn't finish it.

Three vamps crawled around on the ground clutching various body parts. Holy godhead. No wonder I hadn't been able to move. Blood trickled down my neck, but the fang had barely nicked me.

Might not have been the fang at all. Maybe blood was oozing from the spot earth power had pushed through my skin and into the vampire's fang.

I jammed power into the three on the ground, aiming for eyes. Temporary blindness could buy me a lot. The others closed in. I aimed at their eyes too, but they were quicker on their feet.

"Call the seethe," someone shouted.

"You do not want to do that," I gritted.

One launched his body at me, colliding with a thud. It gave me an even shot at his eyes. Unlike the three still floundering in the dirt, his eyes caught fire. It didn't compute. I'd summoned earth, not fire.

The inferno in his eyes spread quickly until he turned into blazing pyre.

I skipped out of the way. What manner of beast was this?

Did the others know they hosted a wolf in sheep's clothing?

Apparently not. The two on their feet turned and ran as if hellhounds chased them. I couldn't do much more damage to the ones on the ground, but I did not want a rematch.

Under any circumstances.

"If you bother me again"—I augmented my voice with magic—"I'll destroy the entire seethe."

Footsteps pounded our way. Typical of mortals. Too little and too late. I didn't need their paltry help any longer.

Sticking around wasn't in my best interest, so I faded into nearby shadows.

If I got lucky, someone would call out a vampire hunter, and the three blind vamps would end up on the wrong end of a silver stake.

I made my way to the castle intent on mapping out my first steps once I took possession.

And was confronted with my second shock since entering Inverness.

Workmen swarmed over the castle. Working on raised platforms, they were clearly constructing a new wing complete with a tower.

Whoever lived there should be packing, not building.

I doubled up a fist and punched the air. James hadn't done a thing. Had he assumed I'd forget?

Another darker thought intruded.

Was he who'd sicced the vampires on me?

It made sense. He had less than zero knowledge about magical creatures. Perhaps he assumed a pack of vampires would be plenty to end one lone werewolf.

Deep in my mind, my wolf howled with laughter.

So long as I was here, I'd find out what I could. Stepping

toward the nearest set of ladders, I swung onto one and climbed to the platform.

A burly fellow turned and scowled. "You ain't part of this crew."

"Right. Is there room for one more?"

He narrowed his eyes. "What are you willing to work for?"

"Food."

He stuck out a hand. "Deal."

I shook it and picked up a trowel. Not much I haven't done, and laying masonry was easily within my skillset. As I worked, I listened—and trolled through minds.

George Gordon, Fourth Earl of Huntly, was the castle's current laird. Earlier earls had been gifted the castle by earlier monarchs. George had decided the castle needed renovating. Toward that end, an entire new wing and tower were in the works. No one knew anything about moving or leaving or relocating.

The longer I worked, the angrier I grew.

Still, I knew better than to do anything other than my job, which consisted of slathering mud between layers of stones. We had to quit soon. It was nearing midnight, and the oil lamps were burning low.

I can see easily, but the men couldn't.

"Quit," rumbled down the ranks of workers, but no one left.

Soon, buckets of nasty gruel were hauled up the ladders via ropes. I hung around long enough to choke down a bowl to establish my credibility. I might tap this source for information again.

Or not.

I'd burn this lot out if James was too much of a pansy to keep to his word.

Once my bowl was empty, I headed for the edge of the platform.

"Where you going?" a deep voice called.

"Down." I didn't even turn around.

"Nope. Servants sleep here. We start again at first light."

The platform creaked. I can move fast when I want; and I was down the ladder and on the ground running before the foreman so much as reached the platform's edge.

"Don't think you'll be coming back," he yelled after me.

So much for keeping that door open.

The city streets were empty. I passed several manor houses that might fit the bill for my assassin guild project, but I wasn't about to back down.

I'd requested Inverness Castle. James had agreed. Meant the castle would be mine. It was just a matter of how.

Curiosity drew me back to where the vampires had jumped me. I cloaked myself in shadows and drew near enough to see three piles of bones. Guess my hopes about vampire hunters had borne fruit. These three wouldn't bother anyone again.

After setting a spell to return me to Edinburgh castle, I considered how to proceed. Threatening James hadn't moved the needle, so further threats would be fruitless.

Not a threat, but a warning was in order.

The more I thought about it, the better I liked it. A warning would give the regent choices. If he chose to do nothing, I'd create a small magical army and take the castle.

Holding it shouldn't prove a problem. None of the peasant class were even remotely loyal. I'd see they were taken care of with no strings attached—if they decided to remain.

Who would I select to assist?

First off, I needed buy-in from a critical mass of mages. I'd covered the bond animal base—sort of. I'd return to their world in a day or so. But selling the idea to anyone beyond Delilah—and Aidyrth—had yet to happen.

I'd done a fair job alienating Delilah. Better to approach Aidyrth next. If the dragon was still in favor of the guild, Delilah would fall into line.

I hoped.

My humble room shimmered into place around me. I stripped off my garments and walked to the servants' bathhouse stark naked. It netted me a few comments, and I sensed desire from both men and women.

I ignored all of it, strode through the door, and stood under a running spray of cold water. Hot water was reserved for nobility, but I didn't care. A sliver of lye soap gave me what I needed to clean the last of the vampire stench off me.

No towels.

Retracing my steps left a trail of water drops and wet footprints. Back in my quarters, I dug out a fresh pair of trousers and a woolen shirt, intent on my last task before leaving Edinburgh Castle forever.

It's never hard to find James. He was in the throne room surrounded by a bevy of naked women. I swear, with all the semen he tosses around, no wonder the castle is overrun with his bastard gets.

It took a while for him to notice me. When he did, he flapped a hand my way. "Return later."

I shook my head. "Nay. I am here now, and here I shall remain until I've said my piece."

"Which is what?" he growled.

"Do you want to send them away first?" I spread an arm to encompass the group of women.

I could hear his teeth grinding against one another from across the room. Finally, he muttered, "Leave us."

Making pretty little noises, the harem bounced out of the throne room, still nude.

James lolled on his back on a bed of furs. His pathetic little dick stood at attention. I've seen five-year-olds who were hung better.

"What?" he snarled. "You have the worst habit of interrupting us."

"I paid Inverness Castle a visit."

He shrugged. "And?"

"No one is preparing to leave."

"Well, they still have a few days."

I covered the distance between us and hunkered so I was at his level. His erection shrank from tiny to non-existent. "They are building a new wing." I kept my voice even. "No one continues to build when they're moving."

"Not my affair—" he began. Color blotched his pale cheeks.

"Aye, it is. We had a bargain. One sealed with your blood. If you welch, you will be exceedingly sorry." I pushed to my feet. "Five more days."

"And then what?" He attempted to bluster.

"And then me and an army of supernaturals will take the castle by force."

Spinning on my heel, I walked out, slamming the door

behind me. Just like last time, the women hovered next to the door. I was certain they'd been eavesdropping, but I didn't care.

I had places to go, people to talk with. And an army of the occult to draw together. Even if James pulled off a miracle, I still needed to come up with a core group of mages to get my vision off the ground.

8

"*Start small,*" my wolf advised as I was taking the castle's steps three at a time heading for my quarters.

Moving was high on my agenda. I have pride— and ethics. I couldn't continue to accept space in Edinburgh Castle if I no longer worked for James. And I'd come close to burning that bridge.

"*Who are you kidding?*" The wolf was back. "*You torched it beyond repair.*"

"*Right you are. As usual.*"

"*Good thing you appreciate it.*"

I nudged my door open with a foot and took stock of my possessions. I've always traveled light. Worked well for me in situations like these where I had to leave quickly.

Efficient as always, I gathered my clothing and personal effects, including a few magical crystals and powders I employ for healing. Everything fit into a valise and two saddlebags. I do own a horse, a stallion stabled with the king's guard.

He'd been a gift from James when I'd rid him of a particularly annoying lord. My first bent was to leave the horse, but a gift was a gift.

Riding out of here would be convenient. I could drape the saddlebags over his back and strap the valise behind my saddle. I swept the room to make certain I hadn't forgotten anything.

"*Where are we going?*" my wolf asked as I trotted down several sets of stairs on my way to a rear door close to the stables.

I'd been thinking about it.

"*Shepherd's cottage on the northern moors.*"

After a pause, the wolf murmured, "*Decent choice.*"

We'd spent a few seasons there before our current stint in James's court. It kept us reasonably close to Inverness and would provide a place to meet other mages. Magic is strong in the Highlands, potent enough to augment my native power. Reason number three it was a solid destination.

I was in the stables preparing Dorian for travel when two of the king's guard stomped in, armor rattling as they walked. Their white garments were soiled, their swords in need of attention.

"The king says you can't leave," one barked.

"Particularly not on that horse," the other added.

I turned to face them and crossed my arms over my chest. "Who's going to stop me?"

Their mouths opened and closed, but neither man could seem to get any words out. To add to their fear, I instigated a partial shift, one where the wolf is visible behind me as a shadowy figure. Their eyes widened; both men fell back a step. One nearly tripped over his sword.

Laughter rolled from me as I turned back and finished tacking up Dorian. I was still laughing when I swung onto his back and trotted out of the stables. James, dimwit of the universe, didn't know what he'd lost in me.

I was the only one of his protectors with an ounce of sense or courage. The only one who'd go to the mat to carry out his orders. The second the two clowns I'd left in the stable thought their precious hides might be on the line, they'd backed so far down they may as well have been in China.

It took us a couple of days to reach Scotland's northwest shoreline. Dorian wouldn't like the next part. In truth, he wasn't overly fond of me and did a lot of stamping and snorting to lodge protests about having a wolf on his back.

Animals know these things.

Awk. Crap. Animals. I was overdue back at their world.

First things first. I'd transport us to the cottage I'd selected, see Dorian was well cared for in pasture with grass up to his belly, and then make all haste to keep my appointed meeting time with the zebra.

I sent a calming spell into the horse's mind. He'd never have tolerated my casting without it. When he came around, we were at the cottage. It wasn't in much worse shape than when I'd seen it about thirty years back. I stacked the saddlebags and valise, covering them with spells so they wouldn't be disturbed. A quick trip to the nearby village rustled up a lad who was keen to make a few pence watching over Dorian for a day or two.

Everything was taken care of.

After retreating to a deserted meadow, I launched my next

journey spell, aiming for the animals' world. At least I wouldn't be late.

The glowing archway shimmered into view, its silvery tones brighter than before. The zebra wasn't standing beneath it tapping a hoof. I took it as a good sign.

"What are we waiting for?" My wolf was near the surface. *"Let's go in."*

"Not the best idea."

Why not?" he persisted.

"Not our house. We will wait until we're invited."

"Didn't happen last time," he groused.

"All the more reason for us to stay put." I sank into a crouch. The animals were a critical element for my assassin guild. Perhaps because of my own dual nature, I believe animals keep mages honest, bring out the best in us.

The wolf yipped agreement.

Good. Meant he'd backed off his storm-the-gates approach.

Time dribbled past. The light in this world didn't change. I didn't see a sun in the sky, or much of anything except the gateway.

What would it mean if no one came?

How long should I wait?

Until something happens. I answered myself.

Nothing to rush back for. I didn't have any meetings or assignments on the horizon.

"Leaving James's court was overdue." The wolf's words surprised me.

"Why?"

"He's a pathetic excuse for a man. How can you work for someone you don't respect?"

I smiled. *"You have a short memory. Most of the monarchs we've worked for haven't exactly been the winners of the world."*

"True, but he's worse than most of the others."

I was starting to wish I'd brought food and drink when the clop of hoofs drove me upright. The zebra appeared, accompanied by a large black raptor riding on her withers.

"Right on time, I see." She neighed approvingly. The raven quorked and took off, flying circles around us.

I bowed and said, "This is important to me."

"Why?"

She was asking questions. I took it as a good sign. "I care about quality. It's important to me to standardize the assassin trade."

She nodded, mane drifting around her neck. "I got that part, but what's different from, say, a hundred years ago?"

"Significantly more botched assassinations. Poisons that end up maiming rather than killing. Sloppy sword work. Overall, a lack of pride. Or perhaps it's placing expediency over excellence. Seems like so many practicing my trade only care about getting paid, not about dispatching their targets quickly and humanely."

"But they're mortals. Why care about them?"

"Many are supernatural beings. My last target was a vampire. It's why the only reasonable approach to organized killing is to recruit mages. Eventually, humans should drop out of the equation. Most of them already have."

She snorted. "Do not be so certain of that, Grigori. Assassination is lucrative. Nothing you can do will dissuade greedy men who enjoy killing."

"If they become a problem, we'll kill them." My wolf commandeered my vocal chords.

The raptor cawed, apparently liking that answer.

"How many magical animals would you require?"

Her question caught me by surprise. "I'm not sure. It would depend on which mages wanted to be part of the guild —and if they already had bond animals."

"Who are you considering?"

"Delilah. Rhiana. Quinn. Kylian."

"They're all bonded," she pointed out.

I nodded. "Aye, but for my guild idea to get off the ground, we'll need a core group of at least a dozen mages. So that leaves eight slots for animals from your world."

"For now," she clarified.

"Aye, for now."

"Would the animals have a choice?"

"Of course they would," I reassured her.

"How would the process work?"

"How do you want it to unfold?" I tossed the ball back her way just like I'd done my first visit here.

She was silent as she considered how to respond. Finally, she said, "When you have a mage in need of a bond animal, you will tell me who it is. Animals will visit the mage in his or her dreams until a potential match is established. As a final step, the mage must come here and meet their prospective mate in person to finalize a tentative bond. If things go well, the pledge will be made permanent after a period of one year."

I held out a hand. She nosed it with her snout. The raven swooped low and pecked my thumb drawing blood.

"Thank you so much." I bowed low.

Her tongue snaked out and licked a drop of my blood.

"Beware," she cautioned. "This arrangement is only viable so long as my kinsmen are treated with dignity and respect."

"Agreed." I dropped my hand to my side.

The raptor resettled himself on the zebra's back. "Our business is complete for the moment," she said. With a swish of her tail, she turned and trotted back through the glowing arch.

Step one was accomplished. I set a spell in motion to return us to the Highlands.

৩৯৩

Total darkness and a brewing storm met me. The wind howled so loud, I heard it from within my journey channel. I'd planned to hunt. We could still do that, but it wouldn't be pleasant. Bad weather tends to drive prey into their dens.

"What do you think?" I asked the wolf.

"About?"

"Feel like hunting, or should I try the public house?"

"Will it still be open?"

I had no idea, but I could usually charm even the sleepiest tavern wench out of a crock of stew and a mug of ale. Since the wolf didn't lodge a protest and insist on shifting, I altered course and brought us out on the far side of a small graveyard.

The town was black as pitch. Made sense. No one burned candles unless they had to. Lamp oil was reserved for the rich. Hunching against pounding sleet and a brisk wind, I hurried to the village's only tavern and pounded on the rough wooden door.

It took at least ten minutes of intermittent thumping

before a young woman with sleepy eyes and a dirty apron tugged the door open.

"Ye'll raise the dead, ye will, with all that racket. What's so important? Did someone die?"

"Will ye allow a poor stranger in out of the storm?" I adopted the local dialect in an effort to blend in. I understood peasants well. If this one thought I was a lord, she'd merrily slam the door in my face.

"'Tisn't free."

"I can pay. Not much, but I have coin," I reassured her.

Reluctantly, she opened the door just enough for me to squeeze through.

"Thank you, miss. Any chance of a bowl of something? Anything will do. I'm not particular."

"Och, so now ye're wanting more than a simple roof over your head."

"If 'tis convenient."

To make it more convenient, I layered compulsion into my words. She'd never notice, and it would hasten making a dent in my empty midsection. She turned away and vanished through a low doorway. Hoping for the best, I sat at a rickety table near the door so she wouldn't have to carry my food quite so far.

When she reappeared a few minutes later, she had a bowl in one hand and a mug in the other. Before setting them down, she cleared her throat and said, "That'll be tuppence."

Reaching into my pocket, I pulled out a coin and dropped it on the scarred wooden tabletop.

She stared at the money, narrowed her eyes, and stood there balancing my food and drink. I understood her dilemma. She wanted to pick up the coin and test it with her teeth to make certain it was real. Both her hands were occupied.

As she shuffled through options, I took a good look at her. Probably not a day over eighteen. Her face still held a trace of youthful roundness. Dark hair spilled down her back, and her dark eyes were clear and bright. Because she was swathed in layers of stained linen apron, it was tough to assess her figure beyond her being on the short side and round.

With a long sigh, she put the bowl and mug on the table and snatched up the coin. To sweeten the pot—and get her to retreat to the kitchen—I dredged one more coin from my pocket.

She grabbed it as well and hustled away before I changed my mind.

I polished off a credible lamb stew in the darkened common room. It lacked seasoning, but the ingredients were fresh. The ale was young but drinkable. I'd have liked another serving of each but didn't want to draw attention myself or push my luck.

When I let myself out the door, the storm had quieted some. It was still raining and sleeting, but the wind had died down. No one was about, so I slipped behind the tavern, hid my clothing under a pile of straw bricks, and shifted. We'd get home faster in wolf form, and I could retrieve my garments the following night.

A startled gasp from behind sent me straight into the air. Twisting, I landed on all four paws, nose twitching. A back entrance to the tavern stood open. The serving wench had a hand over her mouth to stifle a scream.

"Knew there was something off about ye," she hissed and threw my coins into the dirt.

Fuck me.

Talking in werewolf form isn't easy, so I shifted back and faced her buck naked. "Keep the money. I dragged you from your bed. You earned it."

Her breath came in little panting gasps. "Canna. 'Tis tainted."

Usually, mortals annoy me. For some unknown reason, I gentled my voice, added a calming spell, and said, "Did I hurt you? Did I take advantage of you?"

She shook her head once.

"If you didn't trust me at all, you'd never have come out here and confronted me."

"Liliane. Who are you talking to?" A man's gruff voice was followed by heavy tread.

"No one, Da," she called over a shoulder.

I cloaked myself in invisibility. If her father tromped outside and found his daughter with a naked man, there'd be hell to pay.

A burly figure with a tangled black beard pulled the door open and grabbed his daughter's arm. "Run off, did he?"

"There was never anyone here," she insisted.

I gave her credit for standing up to her father.

"Like hell there wasn't." He backhanded her across the face. "Ye're a slut, ye are. High time I married you off afore ye embarrass the family."

Her cheek bloomed red where he'd struck her. It took all my self-discipline not to emerge from behind my spell and pound him into the dirt, but it wouldn't help her cause. If I did that, she'd end up homeless.

He dragged her inside and slammed the door.

It was my cue to get moving. Suddenly, leaving my

clothing was a very bad idea. If Liliane's da was inclined, he'd search the alley for clues come daybreak. I scooped up my discarded items and moved a couple of alleys over to dress once again.

It was dawn, and I was drenched by the time I got back to my cottage.

The straw pallet was more inviting than a king's bed would have been, and I lay on it, covering myself with a pile of tanned hides.

I don't sleep as much as I drift, treading the edges of consciousness. Sun spilling through the cottage's single open window decided things. High time to be up and moving.

I needed reinforcements to secure Inverness Castle. While not assassin work *per se*, still it would be a decent opportunity for several of us to see how we worked together. I may have mentioned assassins are a solitary lot. Creating a guild where we worked in tandem with one another would step on more than a few independent toes.

It pained me, but my first stop had to be Delilah and Aidyrth. I needed to mend any rents I'd created between Delilah and me. Having the dragon's full cooperation would be a huge plus as well.

I'd laid down in my wet clothes, but they were mostly dry now. I traded damp socks for fresh ones and was ready to leave when a timid knock sent me lunging toward the door. When I tugged it open, Liliane stood there next to the lad I'd hired to take care of Dorian.

"Figured it had to be you," she said.

I looked from her to the boy and back. Apparently, they were friends—or maybe lovers. "What do you want?"

I was fairly certain I knew, but it never hurts to ask.

"We won't tell anyone about you," Liliane said and hooked a finger into the sigil against evil.

"If you pay us." The boy finished her thought.

"Blackmail? You're blackmailing me?" The thought was so absurd, so ludicrous, I dissolved into laughter.

The children—and really they weren't much more than that—fell back a few steps, mouths agape.

What? Had they expected me to be so terrified of being exposed I'd agree with anything?

When I could talk again, I nailed each of them with my gaze. "We can do this the easy way or the hard way," I began and inserted a lengthy pause to make certain they squirmed a bit.

Two sets of eyes widened as I trapped Liliane and the lad —really needed to recall his name—in thrall.

"The easy way is you return to the village and say nothing. The hard way is if you can't keep your mouths shut, you'll find yourselves lacking tongues. Maybe fingers too. I'll make certain to strip out a good part of your memories while I'm at it."

"Ye wouldn't," Liliane gasped and repeated the sigil. Her rosy complexion paled.

"Do you want to try me?"

I switched my attention to the boy. "I'm already paying you, and quite handsomely, to care for Dorian. Would you rather I found another for that task?"

"No," he said sullenly.

"Perhaps I will anyway," I mused out loud. "What are you to one another?"

"He's my brother," Liliane mumbled.

Aha. No wonder they'd compared notes so quickly.

"What's your pleasure?" I inquired. "I'm willing to forget this conversation ever happened."

Liliane chewed her lower lip. I could have read her mind, but I waited to see what she had to say. "This house"—she waved a hand—"if ye're not here much. I could clean it if ye'd let me stay."

We'd moved from blackmail to a different sort of bargaining.

"Define stay."

She looked at her feet. "Not all the time. But when I need to get away."

"Da, he gets drunk and has his way wi' her," the lad spoke up.

Liliane punched him. "Ye should be horsewhipped for lying."

My next move wasn't particularly smart, not if I wanted to remain in the villagers' good graces, but I've always had a soft spot for girls in her situation.

"This will not be permanent," I stressed, "but I need to leave for a few days. You may come here as you need to while I'm gone under one condition."

"What?" Liliane was more animated than I'd seen her.

"You must ensure you aren't followed. I do not want your Da to think I'm trading anything for favors if you catch my meaning."

"He won't," the lad piped up. "I ride Dorian out here most days. Lily can take over that task."

I held out both hands. He took one, she the other. While I had hold of them, I crafted subtle alterations in their memories removing any trace of werewolf. They'd remember me, but not what I am.

Both of them shook their heads as I let go. I made shooing motions. "Off with you. Take good care of Dorian."

"The best." The lad mock saluted.

He and his sister took off at a trot for the village. Both were barefoot. Before I ran into any more delays, I summoned a spell to take me to the house where I'd last met Aidyrth and Delilah.

If they weren't there, the wolf and I could track them.

As the spell swept me into its maw, I chafed at how much time everything was taking. Usually, I envision a task, act on it, and move on. I'd never undertaken anything this major before.

Or this complex.

"We're bound to make mistakes," the wolf observed.

Kind of him to use the inclusive pronoun.

"No reason not to keep going," I reminded him.

"Never said it was."

The animals were on board. All I needed were a few mages, and we'd get this project off the ground.

9

When I arrived at the castle, it was deserted. The sun was heading in a westerly direction and reflected off the castle's many windows in crystalline glory. I pushed on the front door, surprised when it opened. Despite my disagreement with Delilah, she and the dragon hadn't barred their doors to me.

The place truly was deserted. I wandered through one well-appointed room after another. Fires burned in every hearth, courtesy of dragon enchantment. On my way through the overstocked kitchens, I helped myself to a few slices of venison, some grapes, and a soft cheese.

Once my belly was full, I returned to the front gates intent on tracking Aidyrth and Delilah. My other option was to wait until they returned. It would give me downtime, but what I craved was action.

I sent tracking threads in every direction waiting for something to ping back at me.

Nothing did.

"Odd," I mumbled.

"Means they didn't use magic to leave," my wolf said.

Sometimes, he makes me feel really stupid. Of course, he was correct.

Since they hadn't used magic to leave, it argued they hadn't gone far. The reason I'd failed to locate them was they'd warded themselves.

What I didn't understand was why. In this truly deserted section of Ireland, no one, magical or otherwise, was near.

"Time for me." The wolf hadn't posed it as a question.

I could have argued. Instead, I hustled out of my clothes and stashed them under a handy brick. The wolf pushed through. He rarely does that, so he must have tuned into something I'd missed.

Loping through the countryside, whiskers twitching and nose soaking up scents, we covered several kilometers before a loch came into view. It was a lovely little body of water with Selkies sunning themselves on rocks in its center. Two males and two females wore their sealskins, but seals would never be this far from the Irish Sea.

The last of the sun's rays dimmed as it sank below the distant horizon.

A muted patina of glimmery power surrounded the group. One waved a flipper my way. Did he know I was more than a wolf?

Time to find out. I morphed back to my human form and hailed the quartet. "Say, have you seen a dragon and a water mage?"

My skin prickled as a truth net circled me. "Are ye friend or foe?" the Selkie inquired.

How to answer? I was still friends with Aidyrth. My status with Delilah was uncertain. "Friend, for the most part. The water mage and I had a slight disagreement during my last visit."

The net's weave tightened around me as it sampled my words for veracity. The Selkie must have been satisfied because he withdrew his spell. I waited, not wanting to appear too eager.

"They passed by here yesterday," he said, "heading that way." A flipper extended in a northwesterly direction.

Nodding my thanks, I shifted back and loped on. Darkness fell quickly, but for once a moon illuminated our way. After a time, a small cluster of stone cottages not unlike mine outside Inverness came into view. Light flickered in the windows of one, but Aidyrth's bulk was a dead giveaway.

Next to her stood a black unicorn. A bigger-than-life brown-and-white eagle flew overhead.

I knew all of them—and the mages they were bonded to.

But why were they here together?

I'd planned to search out Rhiana and Quinn. It was too convenient they were already here. So far, no one had noticed me, but I was still half a kilometer away.

Only the weak post sentries, and no one would ever accuse these bond animals of weakness.

Woofing a greeting, I ran toward them.

"Grigori!" Dorcha brayed and tapped me with her horn. Roland squawked loudly and skidded in for a landing, centimeters from my paws.

"You changed your mind?" Aidyrth managed to convey pleasure and confusion.

Changed my mind about what?

Since I didn't want to hold a complex conversation in garbled speech, I grabbed the point and shifted. Once the magical dust settled, I rubbed the unicorn's dark, silky neck and inclined my head the dragon's way.

When I straightened, I said, "What a wonderful surprise to see you all. Why are you here?"

"A bigger question"—Rhiana strode out of the stone hut and hugged me close—"is why you are." Coal-black curls fell to waist level. Curvy and a decent height, she was an elemental mage. Long ago, her kind was the only mage. They controlled every element until the Celts decided they carried far too much power. Over time, elemental mages were phased out, replaced by those who controlled but a single element. Rather like Delilah being a water mage. In the muted light of the moon, Rhiana's eyes appeared blue, but they'd shade to bronze under brighter conditions.

"Aye. Inquiring minds want to know." Quinn joined her. Over two meters tall, dark hair streamed down his shoulders and back, accentuating the Slavic cast to his features. On a good day, he might pass for human as long as no one noticed his eyes. Like all earth wizard eyes, they're bronze with deep-green centers. I've seen dragons with eyes like his. Aidyrth, for example.

Roland left the unicorn for his bondmate's broad shoulders. "I asked about you. Delilah said you weren't interested in this project."

An uncomfortable sensation stabbed me in the vicinity of the solar plexus. Best not to jump to conclusions. "What project?" I asked carefully, hoping to every goddess I was wrong about what was unfolding.

"Why the assassin guild," the dragon trumpeted. "The selfsame idea you hatched up when you were here last."

Fury scoured me. Why that two-timing bitch. How dare Delilah snatch up my idea and ride with it? Did she think I'd never find out?

A muted bugle told me to cloak my thoughts. And my feelings. How much had Aidyrth uncovered? Knowing how sensitive dragons are, probably everything. She knew her bondmate better than anyone. Being bonded is a lot like being married. It's even true for those like my wolf and me.

The same, yet different, we appreciate each other's strengths and shore up one another's weaknesses.

Running Delilah down would buy me nothing. Standing on ceremony about the water mage stealing my idea, while pretending I was no longer interested, might drive a wedge between her and Aidyrth, which wasn't my intent at all. I wanted a group willing and able to work together. Not one beset with petty infighting and jealousies.

Since changing my mind seemed to be the theme of the hour—and since Delilah was the only one left in the stone cottage—I crafted a plan on the fly. No wonder the turncoat bitch hadn't left the hut. She was afraid her perfidy would come to light.

Not that we assassin mages always got along.

Much of the time, we didn't, which was one of the overarching plusses for forming a guild. "We'll talk," I promised, "but let's include Delilah. After slithering around everybody, I strode into the hut. The door whipped shut behind me. A sound barrier followed.

Delilah was on her feet, hands on her hips, facing me, her

turquoise eyes narrowed to slits. "What are you doing to do?" she snarled.

"Nothing, so long as you cooperate."

"What does that mean?"

"Simple. I tell everyone I changed my mind, and you cede control of the guild to me."

"Like hell I will." She stamped her foot.

"The other option is far less pleasant," I warned. "I'll tell the truth and invite everyone to snare me in a truth net."

Her eyes lost their pinched look. She glided forward oozing pheromones. "We could rule together."

Back on that theme, huh?

"I'm not interested. I don't trust you. It's not the makings of an effective partnership."

"I don't see why not," she simpered, trading pheromones for compulsion.

If she couldn't muscle her way through with sex, she'd opt for magic. Had there ever been a time I'd liked or respected her? Unfortunately, I was still drawn to her beauty.

"Many reasons, but we're not going to delve into them now. What we're going to do is walk outside and join the others before they grow suspicious. And then we're going to map out a charter for the assassin guild."

"I no longer want to be part of it."

My patience snapped. I hauled off and backhanded her. When a red spot bloomed on her cheek, I felt terrible and sent magic to heal the bruised place. "I'm sorry." My voice was gruff. "Shouldn't have done that, but you're acting like a spoiled brat. Aidyrth likes the idea of an assassin guild. She won't want to pull the plug on the idea."

"At least you're right about that." Delilah sounded sullen.

She rubbed her jaw with one hand to underscore what a cad I'd been.

Rather than pointing out what other things I might potentially be right about, I asked, "What was discussed before I arrived?"

She opened her mouth to say something like, "Why should I tell you?" but thought better of it. I saw her internal struggle, eavesdropped shamelessly on her thoughts.

"Mostly, we were catching up," she mumbled. "It's been a while since we've been together. Aidyrth and I had just floated the concept of creating a central agency for all assassin-related work to flow through."

"Mmph. I suppose you were going to run it."

"Something like that, although Rhiana didn't agree."

She wouldn't have. The elemental mage has been a one-woman show for as long as I've known her. I'd anticipated that problem would crop up but hadn't settled on a way to address it.

I gave the door a shove with magic and motioned Delilah through. I might be overreacting, but I didn't trust her behind me. Not that she'd win in a head-to-head battle, but the process wouldn't be pretty, and it would sabotage the upbeat tone I aimed for to get the guild off the ground.

Delilah flounced forward, stopping beneath the low lintel to arrange her features into a pleasant mask. I knew how phony it was, but it would pass if the others didn't dig too deep.

"Aren't the two of you thicker than thieves," Rhiana commented.

"Nah, they should get a room, though," Quinn smirked as

he reacted to residual pheromones wafting around the two of us.

I slugged him in the arm. Roland pecked me; I swatted him but not hard.

"Delilah misunderstood my intent," I told the group. "During my last sojourn here, I began hatching up the idea of an assassin guild and discussed it with Aidyrth and her.

"And then I had to leave to deal with unfinished business in James's court. He promised me Inverness Castle and was busy reneging on the deal."

Rhiana made a snorting sound mirrored by Dorcha, her unicorn. "We shouldn't have much trouble eliminating the current residents."

"Thank you. I could use a spot of assistance. Not that mortals will fight back too hard once they understand who's on the other side."

I blew out a breath sorting what to say next. "Once I was done with James, I stopped by the animals' special world."

"Why?" Dorcha whinnied.

"Because part of my plan for the guild is it will only include mages bonded with animals. For that to be a reality, I needed cooperation from their realm."

"Was it forthcoming?" Roland cawed.

I nodded. "Aye. We have a system in place for any promising unbonded mages to engage an animal."

"You've been busy." Aidyrth huffed steam around me, the dragon equivalent of approval.

You have no idea...

"In any event," I continued, "it's convenient to find you all in one spot. Gathering you was my next objective."

"Why us?" Rhiana arched a dark brow.

"Because I trust each of you and can't imagine a stronger base for the guild." It was almost true. The only one I didn't trust was Delilah. If she was plotting rebellion, it wasn't obvious. If she hadn't been so underhanded, I'd have felt sorry for her. Her bondmate was entranced with the idea, which made it difficult for her to walk away.

Most bonded pairs carry equal weight, but they don't include a dragon. I've never been bonded with one, so I don't know for certain, but I've always assumed the dragon ran the show.

The elemental mage shrugged. "I have to think about this. Been working with Dorcha forever. I'm not certain I'm good guild material. I'm set in my ways. What if I disagreed with one of your edicts?"

She skewered me with eyes that blazed bronze, their earlier blue nowhere in sight.

"We'd talk about it." I adopted a conciliatory tone.

Another shrug. "Talk, schmalk. What if we never found common ground?"

"The only way it would happen," I spoke slowly, "is if you disagreed with an assignment or the method of carrying it out."

"Go on." The weight of her full attention was unsettling, reminding me how powerful elemental mages are.

"If you disapproved of a target—or a methodology—I'd convene the entire group to discuss it, and we'd go with the consensus."

"What if the decision went against my wishes," she persisted.

"Then another mage would carry out the assignment. Unless there was good reason not to pursue it."

Furrows formed in her forehead. "I see."

It was my turn. "And?" I spun one hand in a come-along motion.

"Mmph. I understand, but I do not like it. This is why I've worked alone. I make the hard choices—and live with any consequences."

"There could be advantages," I tossed out.

"Such as?" Quinn jumped into the discussion.

"It would get you out from under dealing with unruly kings and regents." I inhaled briskly, building a structure as I went. "It would ensure standards in our profession."

"What would you do with mages who didn't, erm, live up to them?" Delilah asked.

The sound of her voice surprised me, as did the fact she hadn't asked a trick question to trip me up. "It would be up to the guild," I replied. "I never wanted to install myself as a petty regent. All critical decisions will be made by the group."

"What happens if you don't agree with one?" she persisted.

"I would abide by the consensus."

Aidyrth blew fire skyward. "Fine and well when there are a mere handful of us. What happens as the guild grows?"

"You're assuming it will," I retorted.

"All successful things do."

Her words warmed me. "We needn't make any lasting commitments this evening," I told everyone. "How about if each of us thinks about my proposal. We could reconvene midmorning tomorrow and hash it out further."

"We could," Rhiana agreed. "How does Inverness Castle fit into your plans? Or does it?"

I slapped my forehead with a palm. What else had I left

out? "Good you asked. I'd planned for it to be our first headquarters. If we grow, as the dragon believes would occur, we might end up with several guild houses scattered across this world and others. One of the plusses of Inverness Castle is it straddles a gateway to borderworlds."

"Would we have to live there?" Quinn extended an arm. Roland hopped toward his wrist.

"Of course not. But we'll need somewhere private, a spot we could swathe in spells to conceal our plans."

"Probably not Inverness Castle." Dorcha nudged me with her horn. "Gateway or no, it's in the center of the town. Not private at all."

"We'll still help you clear the current occupants out," Rhiana hurried to add. "But my bondmate is correct. Aidyrth's castle would make a better base of operations."

I glanced at the dragon to gauge her reaction. She nodded, scales clanking, and said, "I'm beginning to appreciate the power of divergent opinions."

An idea took shape. "We'll meet either here or at Aidyrth's midmorning tomorrow. Come armed with plans to capture Inverness Castle. It's not an assassination, but it will offer an opportunity for us to work together no matter what we end up doing with the castle."

"Thought it was yours," Delilah muttered.

"It could be," I replied carefully. "Since I severed my connection with James, I'm more-or-less homeless. For the moment, my possessions are in a shepherd's cottage in the Highlands outside Inverness."

"He'll talk with other regents," Quinn muttered. "Might make them less willing to toss work our way."

"Or more," I countered. "He's not well liked."

"There is that," Rhiana agreed and swung onto Dorcha's back. "See you tomorrow."

"Meet at my home," Aidyrth bugled.

It was as good a point as any to reclaim my wolf's body. I'd been burning through magic to stay warm. *Tomorrow it is,* I agreed and loped into the night. Delilah hadn't pushed for ascendency. It worried me, but not too much. Keeping Aidyrth on her side was critical.

If the dragon knew the full extent of her betrayal, there'd be hell to pay. Perhaps she already did, but if it wasn't kicked to the fore, she'd ignore it.

"Why did you believe this would be simpler than how we do things now?" the wolf demanded.

If I'd been in my human body, I'd have laughed. As things sat, I settled for a long, drawn-out howl. A fat jackrabbit did his damnedest to hop out of the way. One spring and he was ours, jaws crunching through bone and succulent blood streaming down our throat.

We'd feed and sleep. Come morning, we'd meet and plan our first endeavor. If it didn't go well, my idea would die a natural death, and my friends would revert to independently executed assassinations.

It wasn't this batch who concerned me, but all the other poorly trained arrogant folk convinced the assassin trade would make them famous.

"We'll have to make certain claiming Inverness Castle unfolds like a cooperative pack after a herd of fat sheep," the wolf said.

While I appreciated the thought, this had to be a group endeavor, which meant an amalgamation of everyone's ideas. Was I capable of ceding that level of control?

I'm going to have to be, or I have no business taking the guild one step further. A stern inner voice chided me.

"We'll call it a circle," the wolf was back.

"Huh?"

"The guild's name," he clarified. *"It should be the Circle of Assassins."*

"Brilliant!"

If we'd been in separate bodies, I'd have clapped him across the shoulders. I settled for one more leap and another fat rabbit. Hunting was good tonight. It might bode well for the morrow.

10

We slept in a small cave near the creek half a
kilometer from Aidyrth's home. With a full
belly, I ceded dreams to the wolf, who took us
backward in time to the earliest of our kind. No one knows
much about werewolves; we've kept it that way on purpose.
The standard myth that a bite is all it takes to transform
mortal to wolf has provided a convenient smokescreen, as has
the legend we only transform during a full moon.

Anubis, the ancient Egyptian god of death, jumped in on
the heels of the fermented grain that created us. He needed a
small army to shepherd souls to the far side of the veil.
Except he trusted no one. We were a compromise. Because
we respected him, many of us agreed to help. For a time, he
was satisfied, but the world changed. Egypt's power waned
along with his.

Disgusted, he left Earth in search of lands where he'd be
revered again. He did not invite us to come along, not that we

would have. I was just past my first century at that point, so mostly I figured things out on my own. Wolves are pack animals, but part of the transformation to werewolf severed us from that particular bent.

I can impregnate in either form, but, if I breed with a mortal woman, the child won't have a shred of magic. Even prior to Anubis's appearance, we'd decided not to produce new werewolves via either the magical grain or birth. Intelligent of him to agree too many of us wouldn't be wise. For a short while, I feared he wanted to use us to create goddess only knows what type of militia.

It never happened.

After he left, we scattered. It's been over a hundred years since I've met another like me.

Garden variety shapeshifters, yes. Werewolves, no.

In our dream, we ran through a thick, lush pasture with a lissome brown werewolf who led us to still more of our kinsmen. I recognized most of them, and it confused me. Why would I be dreaming about wolves I hadn't thought about in centuries?

"You should come with us," the brown wolf—Alara —woofed.

"Where?" My wolf licked her snout.

The conversation grabbed my attention. Rather than replaying history, I focused on what she had to say.

"We've established our own place," she explained. "The only way to spread the word is through the dreamscape."

"What do you mean?" My wolf's ears pricked forward.

"We don't exactly fit anywhere. We're not mages. We're not like other shapeshifters. Our magic is unique, so we've found a spot we can be ourselves with no worries about being hunted by zealots. Game is plentiful. You should join us."

"Someday. For now, we have a project."

"What kind of project?" Alara asked. "Surely, it can't be more important than establishing a homeland for us."

My wolf whined, uncertain how much to share.

This was a dream, but its impact would extend beyond our wakening.

"We had a homeland once." I stepped in, borrowing the wolf's vocal cords. "It didn't go especially well."

"No one asked you," Alara growled.

Her attitude alerted me she'd left out a whole lot about this "special" place. It was sounding more like a "have to" than a "want to."

"Correct," I replied cheerfully. "No one did."

"Can you tell us where this world is?" my wolf asked.

Alara shook her head. "Not unless you commit to joining us."

"But surely we'd leave there from time to time," my wolf persisted.

Alara didn't reply beyond an ear flick. We can remain silent, but we cannot lie—not to our own kind.

Another red flag.

My wolf inclined his head, murmured, "Anubis's blessing," and turned away.

"Wait!" Alara woofed. "This is important, urgent."

We kept on walking and then settled into a lope. I expected her to race after us. She didn't.

"Something isn't right," my wolf murmured.

"Agreed." An ugly thought intruded. *"Do you suppose someone seized control and they're recruiting us for something?"*

We stopped dead. The dream world splintered around us leaving the soothing babble of the creek. *"It would explain a lot,"* the wolf whined.

"Are you worried?"

"Aren't you?" he tossed back.

I thought about it. *"We haven't had any interaction with other weres for so long I barely remember them. If they got themselves into trouble..."*

"They need help from someone who hasn't yet been snared."

I gave the wolf points for loyalty. *"What do you want to do?"*

"Return to the dream place and find out more."

A sudden chill shot down my spine. An idea followed in its wake. *"This could be our first project."*

"Why first? We've worked on many tasks." The wolf howled and swished his lush black tail.

"Not what I meant. Rather than securing Inverness Castle, which we can do anytime, we could sleuth out what's happening with werewolves."

"But the others are mages, not like us," the wolf protested.

"Doesn't mean they might not want to help."

I liked the idea. It held elements of detective work, danger, and the payoff of assisting fellow magic wielders. Whether an earth mage, a water mage, and an elemental mage would view it in that light remained to be seen. Let alone a dragon.

Dawn was breaking lending the eastern horizon a pearlescent glow. No time like the present to return to the castle, collect my clothes, and settle in with a pot of tea and perhaps breakfast. I'd remain in the courtyard with my tea and food in case Delilah assumed I'd hustled to her side because I'd had a change of heart regarding her proposal.

The morning was crisp and clear. Not dry because nothing ever truly dried out in this part of the world. My paws crunched over ice shards as we covered the distance to the castle. Once we returned to where I'd left my garments, we shifted and I dressed.

No evidence of anyone being awake, except I wasn't aware dragons ever slept. Aidyrth might be out hunting. Or perhaps she'd made a quick trip to Fire Mountain, the dragons' ancestral home. It wasn't particularly easy for the rest of us to access, but dragons command their own journey portals, ones barred to the rest of us.

After a hesitation I let myself inside. The pause had been spawned from my concern Delilah would pounce, but I couldn't let it get in the way. Not if we were going to work together on projects.

I was in the kitchens heating water for tea when Roland swooped through the door and perched on the edge of a nearby table. Quinn appeared next, rubbing his meaty hands together.

"Tea. Grand idea. You're making enough to share, I presume."

"Of course, mate."

The eagle clacked his beak a few times. "Food?" he chirped hopefully.

Quinn turned his gaze on his bird. "Told you to go hunting."

I poured boiling water over a mix of tea leaves I'd selected from bins on the ledge. While it steeped, I took stock of possible breakfast items. The larder wasn't well-stocked, not by castle standards. But then, there weren't any servants here, either.

"Looks like we all need to hunt." I handed Quinn a steaming mug. "Shall we move outdoors?"

"We could. Where's Delilah?"

I shrugged. "Still sleeping?"

"You don't know?" He arched a dark brow.

I snatched up my own mug and led the way out of the kitchen. "Why would I?" I tossed over a shoulder.

After a lengthy pause, Quinn replied, "Sorry. Guess I read things wrong."

I settled on a stone bench in the courtyard. Quinn sat opposite me; Roland took to the skies, cawing dispiritedly.

"What's wrong with him?" I asked quietly.

"Nothing. He was hoping for dragon leavings. They're not fond of entrails, and he loves them."

Rhiana cantered up astride Dorcha. After waving a hello, she jumped down and scooted inside, perhaps in search of her own drink. When she appeared moments later empty-handed, she said, "Not much here to eat."

The whoosh of wingbeats overhead drew my eyes skyward. I'd expected Roland, but Aidyrth flew into view, a sheep and a goat clutched in her mighty jaws. They plopped onto the ground a couple of meters away.

We'd wanted food. Here it was, nicely delivered. I slid a knife from its waist sheath and knelt next to the goat. Quinn got the idea and went to work on the sheep. He had the harder job, since sheep hide is thick and unyielding.

Rhiana grabbed a few sticks of kindling, lit them with magic, and had a glorious fire going by the time we brought meat to her for cooking. Dorcha wandered off to a nearby meadow and grazed happily in grass up to her belly. Roland landed nearby pecking at a good-sized rodent he'd caught before settling in over a pile of steaming sheep innards.

I wanted to float my idea about aiding werewolves, but we all needed to be in the same spot. The dragon had flown off, probably in search of her own meal. Kind of her—and very undragonlike—to provide for us first.

Delilah slithered out of the castle dressed in the same clothing she'd worn the previous evening. Circles beneath her eyes suggested she hadn't slept. A petty part of me was glad. After the shenanigans she'd tried to pull, she shouldn't rest well.

Uncharitable of me. I kicked myself, since I had to move on. A waiflike quality about her drew me in, made me wish things were different. I still cared about her, about our long friendship. But she'd blown things sky high.

Once she'd filched a hunk of goat meat from the top of the cooked stack, she sat near Quinn and mumbled, "Morning, everyone."

Aidyrth dropped out of the sky with a half-eaten sheep in her mouth. She polished off the rest in short order and announced, "Waste of time cooking them. Far better raw."

I grinned. "Aye, but you eat the coat and hoofs and everything."

"Why not?" She bugled and sent steam my way. "Wasting food isn't wise."

Everyone was here. I wiped grease off my hands in a nearby shrub and faced the group. "My wolf and I had an interesting experience last night."

"Oh?" Rhiana set down the stick she'd been using to manage the fire.

"Aye. We entered the dream world and met up with other werewolves."

"Where the fuck have they been keeping themselves?" Quinn asked. "Haven't seen any except you in longer than I can recall."

"How many of you are there?" Aidyrth asked.

I crinkled my forehead in thought. "Not exactly sure, but between forty and seventy or so."

"But that's the same number from forever ago," Rhiana pointed out.

I nodded. "We made a decision not to create more of ourselves. Some of us have probably mated with mortals, but the result isn't another werewolf."

Her eyebrows shot up. Clearly, this was news to her. Not only do mortals not know much about us, neither do our fellow mages. "Interesting," she murmured.

"Numbers aren't the point." I forged ahead. "While we were there, another were said there's now a special world just for us. She invited us to go there but refused to tell us where it is. When my wolf mentioned that surely we'd be free to come and go, she was very closemouthed."

"Sounds suspicious." Quinn drained the remainder of his tea. "Anyone want more?" He waggled his mug.

"I do, but please remain until I'm done."

The earth mage looked surprised. "Why?"

No reason to pussyfoot around. "The wolf and I are concerned someone has established a hold over werewolves. We walked away last night because naught that happens in the dreamworld translates to waking reality. Still, I suspect if we'd taken Alara up on her invitation, we'd have been trapped, unable to leave this new special world."

"What earthly use would anyone have for a pack of werewolves?" Aidyrth trumpeted, followed by, "Hurry this up. I'm still hungry."

"A better question," I shot back annoyed by how dismissive she'd been toward my kinsmen, "is whether the weres require assistance extricating themselves from a bit fat problem."

"I see where this is going," Delilah spoke up. "You want us to come with you to help."

"I thought we were going to capture Inverness Castle," Quinn said.

"We still are," I replied. "But it will still be there tomorrow, next week, or next year. By then, weres could have been completely enslaved.

"Or wiped out."

I'd said what I needed and glanced around at the group.

Rhiana frowned. "I don't know. Our covenant expressly forbids interference."

"With mortal concerns," I corrected her.

"Kind of the same thing." She eyed me. "If we jumped in whenever another type of mage ran into difficulties, we'd be forever snarled in internecine warfare."

"Speaking of warfare, do you have any idea what other type of mage is involved?" Aidyrth trumpeted.

She must be intrigued, else she'd have flown off in search of another fat sheep.

I shook my head. "I could be way off base about all of this. Perhaps my kinsmen really did commandeer their own borderworld for unknown purposes. But Alara was acting very strange. In her own way, I believe she was warning me. When we turned down her invitation, she didn't follow us or lasso us with a holding spell. And she could have."

"I'll be back," the dragon announced and spread her wings. "I think better on a full stomach."

"Same for me. I'll get us more tea." Quinn ambled to his feet.

"Hold up for a moment. We don't have to do this," I said before the group scattered. "We can still choose Inverness Castle. The advantage of digging deeper into what's going on with my kinsmen is it will give us an opportunity to problem solve as a group, a chance to see how well we work as a team when there are a lot of unknowns.

"The castle is easy. Mowing through a bunch of mortals is child's play. It won't challenge us. This will."

Aidyrth's eyes with their deep green centers whirled faster. Flapping her wings, she ran a few paces and was airborne. Quinn headed for the kitchen, presumably to make more tea.

I glanced at those who remained. The more I'd talked about the werewolf problem, the surer I'd become it was the proper choice. If this group didn't agree, I'd take it on by myself.

It would hold up forming the Circle, but I couldn't walk away. Not with the fate of my people hanging in the balance.

"Opening another topic, my wolf had a grand idea," I told Rhiana and Delilah. "He came up with a name for our guild."

"What is it?" Delilah asked.

"Circle of Assassins."

Both women grinned. "I like it better than Assassins' Guild," Delilah said.

"Me too," Rhiana agreed.

"Me three." Quinn's voice, augmented by magic, boomed

from inside the castle.

Roland cawed assent. Dorcha whinnied.

Excellent. We had consensus on our name. It boded well for working together.

Quinn plodded back, a tray balanced between his hands. On it sat a good-sized metal kettle, mugs, and piles of tea leaves. "Help yourselves," he urged and placed the tray on the ground between us.

The sun reached for midheaven adding a spot of warmth to an otherwise chilly day.

Quinn sipped his tea. "Might be fun solving the werewolf problem."

"I was thinking the same," Rhiana murmured.

"Not much assassin work involved," Delilah said.

"You can't know that," I told her. "We might have to fight our way out of a hellish spot. If I'm correct, and darker magic is involved, all your assassin skills will be needed."

"Let's see what my bondmate wants to do," she countered. "If she's in agreement, of course I'll be part of it."

"Looking promising," my wolf said from the spot where he lives within me.

It was, but I've learned not to assume anything. We needed the dragon on board. This would be our first group effort, which meant no one sat it out.

Aidyrth didn't return for half an hour. When she scudded out of the skies, she had a cow in her jaws and looked pleased with herself. Rather than tucking in to polish off the carcass, she said, "I was busy. Tapped into our dragon communication network. Werewolves have been a hot topic these days."

I leaned forward. Her next words would clinch this one way or the other.

She puffed steam my way. "Anubis is back from wherever he went. He's reclaiming his charges, which wouldn't be alarming except he's joined forces with the Morrigan, and—"

"Wasn't she imprisoned in Fire Mountain?" Rhiana cut in.

Aidyrth clacked her jaws together so hard, the sound of double rows of teeth clashing against one another was deafening. "Anubis stopped by to pay us a visit. I wasn't present, but this is the tale I was told. We interpreted his visit as a courtesy to alert us he had returned."

Another clack, louder than the previous one.

Delilah pushed upright from her seat and stood next to her bondmate, offering moral support.

"What he was really doing," Aidyrth continued, "was sneakily freeing the Battle Crow. He'd requested to visit her under the guise of her being an old friend. That part was correct. What we didn't know was just how close they were. He remained with us for another day, feasting and regaling us with tales of his travels. During that time, no one thought to check on the Morrigan."

"Let me guess," I inserted dryly. "When someone did look in on her, she was long gone."

More clacks.

"But dragons are the best trackers ever." Delilah stroked her bondmate's scales.

"In this instance, we failed. Not that my kin have given up, but for now, the trail is more than cold." She aimed her whirling eyes right at me. "If your project will get me closer to Anubis, I'm all in, wings, scales, and teeth. Other dragons will join us."

Delight swamped me. This was getting better and better. "When do you want to leave?" I asked everyone.

"The sooner the better," Aidyrth trumpeted.

"Where will we start?" Rhiana asked.

I'd had time to consider just that question. "My wolf and I will return to the dreamscape, but you will mark us with magic so we're readily found. This time, we'll agree to accompany Alara—or whoever approaches us."

Aidyrth clapped her forelegs together. "Perfect. Simple. Clean. Once we know where you are, we'll swoop in and—"

"And what?" I angled my head to one side. "Severing Anubis's hold over werewolves won't be simple."

"Why not? He abandoned you." The dragon puffed up her scaled chest.

I took a deep breath. Either I held nothing back, or we had no partnership. "Because most of us willingly ceded a leadership role to him. At the time, we were flattered a god wanted us as minions."

A symphony of "ooohhhs" and "explains a lot" ran through the group.

"Dealing with him won't be impossible," Rhiana pronounced. "Granted, a shade more difficult."

"We can do this, now we know what we face." Quinn clapped me across the shoulders.

"Do you have..." Rhiana ran through a list including griffon blood, crystalline quartz, amethyst powder, and several other arcane items.

"Most of it," Delilah replied and beckoned. "Follow me. You can cull through my collection."

Aidyrth spread her wings.

"Where are you going?" I asked.

"To gather a few allies to our cause. Back soon."

I should have kept my mouth shut. Truly I should have,

but I've never been especially diplomatic. "Are you certain you can trust them?"

She whirled. Instead of steam, she showered me with fiery ash. "How dare you question me," she hissed, tongue snaking outward.

Not a time to back down. "Can you be absolutely certain Anubis didn't have help freeing the Morrigan from within your ranks? Riding herd on her must have been a total pain in the rump. I don't recall exactly how dragons ended up babysitting her, but it had to engender resentment."

More ash rained down. My garments smoldered in a few spots. I resisted the urge to pat the burning places.

"If I didn't want what you have, I'd flatten you on the spot, werewolf."

I considered thanking her for not putting me in an even tougher position but didn't. "Since you're going to be talking with other dragons, ask what they think about my theory. I'd love to be proven wrong, but we have to be cautious. If Anubis knows we're gunning for him, I'll be walking into a trap."

She leapt skyward, wings flapping furiously.

"Never were much for tact, mate," Quinn observed dryly.

"There wasn't a way to say what I did tactfully," I gritted. I'd had it up to here with criticism.

His features took on a thoughtful cast. "Perhaps not." Gesturing at the pile of meat, he urged, "Eat. Hard to know when your next meal will be."

I took care of my smoldering tunic and dug in. The wolf part of me has a deeply pragmatic side. Food would feed my magic, and goddess only knew how much I'd need to waltz into Anubis's new realm and not end up fodder for the god.

11

Somehow it was midday and then the middle of the afternoon. The pleasant sunny morning had shaded to a steady drizzle. Quinn, Rhiana, Delilah and I retreated to the covered portion of the courtyard. Aidyrth returned with two other dragons, one green and the other black. She didn't say another word about my cheekiness, so maybe the other dragons had corroborated my suspicions and she was too embarrassed to admit it.

"Are you ready?" Quinn asked me.

"Depends. Are you certain you've all marked me sufficiently with your magic to make me findable?"

My flesh stung as everyone tossed still more beacons my way. They had to be cautious and bury them so deep my essence overshadowed half-a-dozen types of non-werewolf magic. I'd argued for being marked by only one or two of them, but I'd been overruled.

If Anubis suspected I wasn't exactly what I'd always been,

he and the Morrigan would strip me to my bones, discarding magical layers as they went.

"Test your links," Aidyrth bugled.

Another round of jabs jostled me. They hurt, but I remained stoic.

"We will follow as we can," Rhiana explained for the dozenth time. "As soon as you leave the dreamscape, we'll do what we can to be close enough to break through quickly."

Irritation spilled through me. No one had fussed over me since I was a boy. "Do not overreact," I growled, sounding a lot like my wolf. "If you come racing in like a supernatural cavalry too soon, we'll have done all this for naught since I won't know anything more than I do right now."

"Not true," Aidyrth corrected me. "We'll have recaptured the Morrigan."

"Can't we just kill her?" the green dragon muttered.

Aidyrth sent a river of flames his way. "If we could have, we would have."

I didn't need to hear any more. With a jaunty wave, I took off for my spot near the creek. It had proved an efficient conduit to the dreamscape before. No reason it would act any differently when the wolf and I retired there for an afternoon nap.

As I loped along, the various magics within me clunked into place. I felt different. How could I not, carrying so many bits and pieces of foreign enchantment. Hopefully, no one would dig too deep.

"I don't have good feelings about this," the wolf muttered.

I had my own spate of doubts, but giving voice to them might breathe life into a host of unpleasant possibilities. Better to remain upbeat, optimistic.

Despite all the effort we'd put into planning, I asked, *"Do you want to back out?"*

It took a while before he answered. *"No, but this won't be as simple as everyone expects. How could it be? He did something to Alara to enable her ability to lie."*

I hadn't considered that aspect. *"She didn't go out of her way to convince us,"* I reminded him. *"When we said no, she didn't run after us."*

"True. So part of her mind must still be her own."

What had her mini-insurrection cost? Maybe nothing. Maybe a lot. I'd find out soon.

I heard the brook's song before it came into view. Fat rain drops plunked into the water, adding to the chitter of waves over several rock cascades. After ducking into the cave, I stripped out of my clothes, tucking them off to one side, and let the transformation take me.

Wolves drift into sleep far quicker than mortals. Our eyes were no sooner closed than the dreamscape burst from a dark sending and snared us. We emerged in a different spot from last time. This place was rugged, surrounded by snow-capped peaks. Chilly air gusted this way and that.

We could have holed up and waited, but it might appear suspicious. The wolf apparently agreed because he took off at an easy pace, half trotting, half running depending on obstacles in front of us.

Unlike last time, I didn't sense a soul, which wasn't unusual. Most of our trips to the dreamscape we hadn't run into anybody. Still, if Anubis and the Morrigan had hatched a plot to capture all the werewolves, leaving me out made no sense.

The skies shaded from gray to a deep blue. Fluffy clouds marched along pushed by the wind.

"Thoughts?" the wolf spoke in our special shielded mind speech. I wasn't at all certain it would be hidden from Anubis. I'd never tested it since he vanished during my youth.

"Once we've rested, we'll return." My words were innocuous enough to mean damn near anything.

The dreamscape lacks day-night cycles. Each trip is slightly different. This time, we had mountains. Last time, we'd run through pasturelands. I sent seeking magic in an arc once again but didn't come up with so much as a trace of anyone ever having been here.

Seemed odd since the dreamscape belongs to all of us.

We stopped next to a partially frozen lake; the wolf flopped onto the ice, soaking in its coolness through his belly. We couldn't remain much longer without arousing suspicion. Even though my magical search came up dry, I couldn't shake the impression someone was watching us.

"Time to go back," I said.

I felt the wolf's uncertainty through our connection but remaining here was futile. If someone was going to show up, we'd have seen them by now. Had I been blackballed after rebuffing Alara? If so, it would put a crimp in the dragons' plans to snatch the Morrigan and return her to her cell—or wherever they kept her.

The wolf clawed toward wakefulness. Once we passed a certain point, we'd leave the dreamscape, trading it for the cave we'd left near Aidyrth's castle. All spells contain a moment where the magic wielder is vulnerable to outside influence. This one was no different.

The transition began, but then it went sideways. Instead

of leaving, the ice broke beneath our body, sucking us into very cold water. We were near shore; it should have been shallow, but it dragged us down at an alarming pace.

The lake—or whatever it was—had no bottom. Must not have been a lake at all but illusion set to trap us. Shock ceded to panic. Outrage overshadowed everything.

How dare they?

"Who're they?" the wolf muttered as he batted his paws trying to grab anything to slow our descent.

I started to force a shift, but the wolf's body was better suited to our predicament. He sucked water into our lungs, sorting air from the liquid. I reined in my control-freak tendencies and let him manage. We'd quit tumbling end over end, but we were still sinking.

I pushed power into a journey spell and kindled it. For the briefest of moments, our liquid home shimmered and shuddered. I poured more effort into my spell. If we could just break free—

Power whipped around pounding us. The wolf yelped, the sound absorbed by cold water. We jolted from side to side until the magic I'd tossed into the journey spell ran down. I tried to reel it in—to shorten our misery—but once it's deployed, magic is tough to recall.

"Do not do that again," he shouted.

"No concerns on that front." I feel whatever he does, and our body smarted from the backlash of our magic turned against us.

Someone was pulling the puppet strings. Escape wasn't within the scope of my magic, so we'd have to wait this one out. It went against the grain. I'm a mage of action, not one who gracefully accepts whatever the universe doles out.

Could I figure out where we were? In pursuit of knowledge, I sent out subtle threads. It took my mind off being trapped.

"Don't even think that," the wolf snapped and clawed at the water. It didn't do any good. Nothing to grab onto.

Information pinged back at me. The water was, indeed, an illusion. An idea bloomed. Rather than a journey spell, I'd funnel magic to break us out of here. Goddess only knew where we'd end up, but if we didn't do something, we'd spend the rest of forever in freezing water. Eventually, lack of food would take its toll; our magic would fade.

Truth in my thoughts lit a fire under me, but this time I told the wolf what I was about to do.

"Not a good idea," he retorted.

"Do you have a better one?"

"Aye. Eventually, we'll get to the bottom."

"If this was a body of water, that would be true. It's not."

"You can't know that."

I swallowed irritation. We were in this together, but it was one time when our shared existence was a liability. *"I examined our situation. The lake isn't real."*

"Feels real enough."

"It's how illusions operate. I need you to trust me on this one."

"I told you I had a bad feeling about this before we left Earth."

"So you did." I paused to emphasize my next words. *"If we wait too long, we won't have enough enchantment to break free. And certainly not enough to face whatever awaits us on the far side of this fake body of water."*

The wolf growled in protest, but we were a team.

"Are you in agreement with me breaking us out of here?"

"Not really, but you'll nag until I say yes."

If we'd been in our other form, I'd have smiled. Not wanting to waste any more time, I gathered power into an arc and heaved it at the spot that had seemed weakest to me when I'd done my data gathering.

The wolf quit beating the water with his paws to maximize all our resources. I girded myself for an unpleasant backlash and gave it everything I had. If this didn't work, we were in deep trouble.

If Anubis—or whoever—knew enough to target me, they knew I had allies. It was why they'd chosen water as a medium to snare me. It dampens magical emanations. Even if Quinn, Rhiana, and the others hunted for me, they'd run into one dead end after another. Aidyrth might have better luck. Her magic was stronger, but either no one was worried, or they'd tried and failed to locate us.

The only water mage was Delilah, and I knew full well how she felt about me. She'd consider it a convenience if I failed to return.

I pushed wave after wave of power in a straight line, instructing them to bypass currents and other impediments the water produced. The wolf propelled us along the path of our magic. At first, I almost told him to stay put, but his instincts are sharper than mine.

So far, there'd been no backlash. Either we were playing right into our enemy's hands, or they couldn't subvert my spell. The wolf's breath came in panting spurts, the water cold on inhale and warm and frothy on the exhale.

There might be no backlash, but nothing else was happening, either. Except me draining our reservoir to bedrock. I considered calling this a failed experiment, but

I've always had a stubborn side. Losing isn't a word in my vernacular.

Earlier, I'd labeled the wolf stubborn. He came by that trait honestly. Immersed in my own obstinacy, I doubled down. If I crashed, this would kill us. Converting water to breathable air takes magic. Leaving the wolf bare minimum, I dug deep.

One more burst. All or nothing.

In a blaze of brilliance, the water vanished. Not so much as a puddle remained. The wolf's sides heaved as he sucked air into our lungs and spit out water. We stood in the midst of a small glen with silver tree boles surrounding us. Red leaves fluttered. Violet-tinged skies held an orangish sun.

Where in the hell were we? No land I'd ever frequented.

Raucous cawing raised hackles along the wolf's neck and back. Time to shift, so I pushed through a hasty transformation in time to see an enormous black crow waddle from between two trees.

As tall as me, her beak clacked ominously.

"Well met, Morrigan," I said. "Or not."

"Good guess, werewolf. I already know who you are. Anubis said you couldn't be captured." More cackling until she sounded more like an oversized chicken than a crow. "I won that bet."

Time to play dumb. "Why capture me? I'd have come willingly. When we entered the dreamscape, I was hunting Alara so she could tell me more about the new werewolf world."

"Do. Not. Lie. To. Me."

The crow took on a glistening aspect and split into three women. All wore sheer white gowns and had long, shiny black hair. They converged on me, reaching with long-nailed hands.

Should have remained a wolf. She wouldn't have tried to seduce him. Pivoting this way and that, I leapt out of their way. They changed direction and tried again.

I summoned fire and created a burning ring around me, unsure if they could cross it. Every once in a while, you get lucky. If fire wasn't the Morrigan's nemesis, she'd have escaped the dragons' home long since.

The three goddesses attempted to breach my line, whining in pain when the fire burned them. I adopted an injured tone. "I came to see the werewolves' new home. If it's not here, I may as well leave."

Never mind, leaving was beyond the reach of whatever magic remained to me, power that was quickly being devoured by the fire. With no warning, the goddesses morphed back into the crow.

I cut the magic fueling the fire; its flames guttered and died.

She clacked her beak and stared at me with her dark, avian eyes. "Come with me. You may as well be with the others."

Cryptic.

Other what? Werewolves?

I strode after her wishing for my clothes and boots.

My nose twitched. I smelled werewolves, and more too. Not the clean, unfettered scent most of us carry but a sickly sweet undertone. I slowed my pace and ran into a barrier behind me.

Forward was the only direction allowed.

Did we keep going and let her toss us into an iron cage—

or however she was holding my kinsmen? Or did we make a break for it? I'd tested a journey spell inside the water illusion. One might work better here.

"Don't fall behind," she cawed over one beefy feathered shoulder.

She'd noticed my laggardly pace.

I might not have found out much about Anubis's plans, but if the dragons showed up now, they could grab the Morrigan, and—

The bird whirled. Far quicker on her clawed feet than I'd have imagined possible, she stalked toward me.

Fuck. Should have warded my thoughts, but I'd assumed she wasn't paying attention.

Wrong. She had me where she wanted me.

Not knowing what would come next, I reached for my links with the fledgling Circle of Assassins and ignited every one of them.

"You traitor!" she screeched.

"Since when did I declare loyalty to you?" I snarled and ducked moments before she'd have slashed her beak across my skull, probably fracturing it. The wolf took over. No longer vulnerable bare flesh, I was fur and fangs and claws.

Roaring a challenge, he rose on his hind legs to meet her attack.

12

In an amazing show of courage, the wolf flew through the air and fastened his jaws around the Battle Crow's neck. Blood geysered as he severed the carotid artery. We couldn't kill her, but maybe we'd slow her down. At least the wolf was using brute strength rather than magic.

Where were the others? They should have heard me.

I hate being dependent on anyone else. Hate it. But in this instance, with our magic running low, I needed assistance.

Blood coated the wolf's snout and squirted into his eyes. He blinked to clear his vision. We were suspended in the air as he hung on, powerful jaws cutting deeper by the moment.

I hoped he cut her fucking head right off. Not that she couldn't regenerate it. Any magical creature that can shapeshift can rebuild lost parts. Including me, so long as I have enough magic stashed away.

She batted at the wolf with her enormous wings, but he'd

wisely fastened himself in a spot she couldn't reach him. Unless she switched things up.

The crow transformed into three women again. We were only clinging to one of them. The others vaulted toward their sister, hands curved into claws suspiciously like the Battle Crow's.

I've often cursed my inability to be in both shapes at once. It would have been so handy to detach my body from the wolf's and meet the goddess's attack. No fire stymied them this time.

We've fought multiple enemies before. Time for a strategy shift.

The wolf chomped through the neck he had in his jaws. The goddess's head hung by threads of skin before falling to the ground. Meanwhile, the wolf whirled and charged one of the others. They shrieked like Banshees. Who knew? Perhaps they were distant relatives.

It's tough to be on the sidelines. I wanted to orchestrate our offensive, but screeching instructions would be counterproductive. The wolf needed all his attention, and, of the two of us, he's the more skilled warrior.

Humbling to admit.

He grappled with one of the women, rolling on the ground as each worked to inflict damage. The wolf had a clear advantage: bigger teeth. The goddess bit his foreleg. He took advantage of her single-minded concentration to wrap his other foreleg around her and close his jaws around the back of her neck. Vertebrae crunched beneath his strong jaws.

Blood poured from her open mouth.

He let go and lunged for the last woman. Just before he reached her, she vanished.

Damn it.

I grabbed the point and reclaimed my body intent on constructing shielding around the two ruined bodies before they disappeared too. So long as we held onto them, the Battle Crow couldn't go far.

At least I didn't think she could.

Bugles announced the imminent arrival of dragons. I dragged the bodies next to one another and tossed shackles around them. I wasn't elegant. A junior mage could have done a better job, but speed was essential.

"Where is she?" Aidyrth trumpeted. Her bulk burst through from somewhere. One moment, the odd sky was clear, the next, she swooped down and skidded to a halt next to me. Two other dragons followed, the green and black ones I'd met near her home.

"Here's part of her." I pointed at the bodies.

The dragon raked them with fire. "Pfft. You fell for the oldest trick in the book. Those are illusion."

"Are you sure about that?" I didn't want to reel in my magic for fear they'd vanish like the third manifestation. And then we truly would have nothing.

Aidyrth turned on me, eyes whirling. Indignation oozed from every scale. "How dare you question me, werewolf."

In for a penny, in for a pound. She was already angry. "Do illusions bleed?"

She flipped her head around and examined the severed neck, the head, and the body with the broken vertebrae once more.

The black dragon stomped forward, tongue flicking this way and that. Who the hell knew what he was doing. Syllables rolled from his mouth, harsh and discordant. The dragons' tongue is one of the few languages I didn't understand much of.

I caught a word here and there, but not enough to put anything together.

All three dragons hovered around the bodies, tongues testing the air. If they had some sort of magical sensory apparatus in them, it was the first I'd known about it.

"*What are they doing?*" my wolf asked.

"*No idea.*"

Aidyrth bugled. The other two joined in. Power flowed amongst them, strong magic that made me jealous. Shiny silver cord appeared from between the black dragon's scales. Aidyrth snatched an end with her taloned foreleg. When it was long enough, the other dragon grabbed hold. Between the two of them, they wrapped it around the remains of the women.

My interest was certainly piqued. Apparently, Aidyrth's blanket statement that I'd been hornswoggled wasn't true. The rope glowed so brightly I shielded my eyes. More dragonspeak.

The ground heaved beneath our feet, once and then again. A pit formed around the bodies, sucking them downward.

Fire shot from three mouths immolating the remains. The pit didn't even slow down. The dirt beneath the dragons' immense hind feet began to crumble too. I felt the pull of a magical vortex. Memories of my watery trap slammed into me.

"Watch out!" I yelled.

The dragons bellowed outrage. Who knows if they heard me?

I scuttled back beyond the vortex's magnetism. I didn't have enough power left to rescue myself again.

As quickly as it had formed, the pit closed over taking the bodies with it. The glowing dragon rope flew skyward. Whoever was managing this shitshow wasn't interested in anything dragonesque.

Aidyrth spread her wings and yelled, "Get on. We're leaving."

Breath boiled from me. Another confrontation, but I had to proceed carefully. I needed the dragons no matter how they felt about werewolves.

The black and green dragons trudged close, clumsy on land. "At least I got this." The black dragon held out the severed head. "Should create a small amount of angst."

"Nice move," Aidyrth bugled and stared at me. "Why aren't you on my back?"

I forced myself to meet her whirling gaze, no easy proposition. "Before you got here, I was following the Battle Crow—"

"Why didn't you call us sooner?" Smoke shot from her jaws, making me cough.

"Wouldn't have mattered. She knew the second I kindled all the links."

"Because you weren't careful," the black dragon pronounced.

"Can we kill him now?" my wolf spoke up.

"Like to see you try." Instead of smoke, fire headed my way. I erected a hasty shield. It wasn't very effective—not much magic left—but it protected my skin from third degree burns.

Damn it. We were getting off track. Before we returned to

my concern about the other werewolves, I asked, "Are the others coming?"

"Who do you mean?" the green dragon asked.

"Quinn, Rhiana, Delilah, Dorcha, and Roland."

"They're waiting, in case we require them," Aidyrth replied.

"This was a dragons' quest," the black dragon clarified.

In their minds... In mine, it had been an opportunity to work as a group.

"Will you explain why you're not on my back?" Aidyrth snorted fire. "Or forget the explanations and just do it."

"Before you got here"—I started over—"I was following the Morrigan. I smelled werewolf, but not healthy ones. She imprisoned my kinsmen. I don't want to leave without them."

"How is that our problem?" Aidyrth folded her forelegs across her scaled chest.

"It's not. Not directly, but we're allies. It didn't work well, but at least I tried to deliver the Battle Crow."

The green dragon turned away, nostrils twitching and tongue out. "I don't smell any werewolves except you."

Crap. Had she moved them already? I sneezed to clear my nostrils of smoke and ash and trotted a few meters from the dragons sniffing all the while. My wolf's nose is far more acute. When I didn't smell anything, I asked him to give it a try.

"Won't work in your body."

I knew that.

Transformations require magic. If we shifted again, there'd truly be nothing left. I'd smelled werewolves in this body before, but no longer. After trotting back to the dragons, I said, "She could have warded them. Could we proceed perhaps a kilometer in the direction she and I were walking? If we don't find them, I'm good with leaving."

"Get on," Aidyrth snapped.

Had she not heard me? Or was this her way of saying no?

"These are our new companions; we should trust them," the wolf observed.

"At least one of you has wisdom," Aidyrth sneered.

My wolf was right. If I didn't trust the dragons, particularly Aidyrth, I had no business forming a guild she'd be part of. Delilah had proven duplicitous, but the dragon hadn't.

Using her scales as an assist, I crawled onto her broad back and draped my legs down both sides of her neck.

"Better," she said. "Now, which way were you walking when you smelled your kinsmen?"

I pointed.

She spread her wings, beat them a time or two, and we were airborne. "Simpler to look this way," she said. "Employ your psychic senses to penetrate possible warding."

On to the next hard part. They just kept on rolling. Admitting weakness doesn't come easily to me—or probably to anyone. After clearing my throat, I said, "I would, except my magic is depleted."

She craned her neck around, eyes whirling in what might have been surprise. "Why? What happened?"

"It's a long story. I'll fill in the details later. We were snared in a water illusion. Took everything we had to break free."

"I see. No wonder you didn't summon us sooner."

Feeling useless, I scanned the countryside below. The other dragons flanked us.

"Open your magical center to me," Aidyrth commanded.

I'd never shared power with anyone. Uncharted territory, but my wolf has good instincts. He'd encouraged me to trust. So far, it was working out. I felt the dragon's ungentle probing behind my breastbone and lowered my defenses.

Magic spilled into me, robust and welcome, rebuilding my resources. I opened my third eye and ear and focused intently on the land flowing beneath Aidyrth's wings.

"Thank you," I murmured.

"Self-serving on my part," she replied. "You're more attuned to werewolves than I am."

Self-serving or not, it was still generous. I shut my earth eyes and poured magic into hunting for my kinsmen. Try as I might, nothing alerted me.

"Could we please turn around?" I asked. "Overfly the same route. If we can't find them, they're not here."

Aidyrth banked and turned. The other dragons matched her movements in an aerial ballet. I opened my psychic senses as wide as possible, barely breathing in my attempt not to miss anything.

We were nearly back to where the pit had absorbed the Battle Crow's remnants when the faintest of faint alterations in my search gave me hope. "Below us," I said.

Iridescence spilled from the dragon, painting the land. Sure enough, a spot off to one side sucked up her magic, leaving a hole.

"Still have that head?" Aidyrth asked the black dragon.

"Of course," he bugled back.

She nodded briskly. Scales rattled. "Excellent. We have something they want, and they have something we want. Should be straightforward."

I chose not to remind her of her initial assessment regarding the various body parts I'd slapped a shield over.

All three dragons banked and wheeled, clearly intent on landing. Usually, I map out a plan, but I'm not a dragon. If I held their level of enchantment, I'd be more comfortable waltzing in anywhere and making demands.

"Anubis might be there," I reminded Aidyrth.

She might have shrugged her shoulders. Or it could have been wings beating. Regardless, she wasn't impressed.

Magical creatures have a hierarchy. Dragons view themselves sitting at the top of the heap. Werewolves have always been lumped in with other shifters at about the midway point, stronger than some, weaker than others.

A jolt ran through me as we landed damn near on top of the area that had sucked in the dragon's magic. I prepared to jump down.

"Don't," Aidyrth cautioned.

I bristled. I might not be the most robust mage, but I fight my own battles.

"Save your misplaced pride for another time," rolled through my head.

Before I reacted—by jumping down, anyway—all three dragons bugled a challenge laced with compulsion. The black dragon held out the captive head. Its eyes opened and shut; so did its mouth.

Disturbing. Was it calling for the Battle Crow? Or was the Crow calling her own, instructing her in some way we weren't privy to?

I kept my eyes trained ahead, staring at the place I expected the Morrigan to pop out. Or Anubis.

I'd met him a few times long, long ago. Would it confer

power over me? The idea was so disquieting, I gathered my newly resurrected magic into a shield.

Aidyrth sensed what I was about and added to my efforts. When she was done, a fortress surrounded me. Except I didn't want that kind of help. It suggested I wasn't capable of taking care of myself. Not the time to complain, not after she'd shared magic with me.

The dragons plodded closer to the break in the weave of reality, bugling all the while. Bending, Aidyrth shoved both forelegs into the spot. It swallowed them until she pushed outward. A wrenching, grinding howl filled the air. Everything altered as the barrier separating us from what I knew had to be there collapsed.

The stench of sick werewolves hit me full in the guts. Sweetly rotten and riddled with decay. Heedless of warding or the dragons' admonition to remain on her back, I leapt down and hit the ground running toward an enormous iron cage.

My wolf howled outrage. *"Let me out."*

"Not yet. We need my hands. And my magic."

He subsided to growls and snarls but didn't fight me for ascendency.

The dragons were closing on us from behind.

The distance to the cage was foreshortened. It took me longer to reach it than I'd expected. Most of my kinsmen wore their human bodies. Alara wriggled through a tight knot of bodies and stopped a meter from the iron bars. She was naked. Tangled copper-colored hair streamed to waist level in clumps and tangles. Medium height, she'd once had curves, but her body was reduced to skin stretched over bones.

"What?" she snapped. "Was my warning not obvious? Not sufficient? Now you'll be trapped with the rest of us."

"Look behind me."

"Nothing's there. You're delusional."

A glance over one shoulder showed three dragons. Why couldn't Alara see them?

Aha! They'd concealed themselves. The Battle Crow would drill through any illusion. Anubis, too. Perhaps. I didn't know him well enough to measure his ability. But a god is a god.

Not addressing her delusional comment, I said, "I understood your message full well. I'm here to rescue you."

"Pfft." She flapped a bony hand. "If it didn't take so much energy, I'd laugh."

Her eyes widened. She fell back a step—and ran into the group of weres behind her. Some were so weak, others held them upright. My first guess was the dragons had dropped their cloaking spell.

The black dragon stepped forward holding the head he'd captured between his forelegs. "We have come to parley," he trumpeted. "But we will not remain long."

"Aye," Aidyrth cut in. "If you do not appear within a count of ten, we will be gone from this place, and you will never see your head again."

Would it work?

I haven't spent much time around gods and suchlike, but they're an arrogant, entitled bunch. Pride might keep the Battle Crow from popping into view. Depended how important the head was to her.

The dragons trumpeted in synchrony. "Ten. Nine. Eight. Seven..."

Raucous crowing interrupted their countdown. The Battle Crow strode through a portal. Wings quivering, she hovered and made a snatch for the head. The black dragon yanked it beyond her reach.

She flew higher. The dragon spread his wings and fixed his whirling gaze on her. In an aerial contest, the Crow would lose, and she knew it.

She snapped her beak. "Fine. Be that way. Unhand my property. This moment. I am not in the mood to play games."

"Neither are we," Aidyrth replied. "Free the werewolves, and the head is yours."

The Crow tossed her black-feathered head. "Name another price."

"There is no other," I said firmly.

She rounded on me. Perhaps she hadn't noticed me standing in the dragons' shadow. "You," she shrieked. "Naught but trouble." Black forked lightning shot from her talons.

Aidyrth short-circuited it with dragonfire. "If you do that again," she said evenly, "we will leave. There is only one deal to be made here. And you have the next minute to make up your mind."

"You're bluffing. He"—she pointed squarely at me—"won't leave without his people."

"Today, I will," I told her. "Doesn't mean I won't plan another attack and return."

"Without your head," the black dragon tacked onto my words.

"Aye, the head is a onetime inducement," Aidyrth purred. "Thirty seconds left. What will it be?"

The Battle Crow cawed like a scalded cat, her outrage so palpable it rained from her in sheets of twisted power. Holding out a front leg, she said, "Deal. Hand it over."

"Nay," the black dragon said. "Free the were people first."

"How do I know I can trust you?" the Crow simpered.

Fire flew from the black dragon's mouth, joined by fire from the green dragon. It danced around the crow but didn't singe so much as a feather. "If you say one more word impugning our honor, we won't spare you next time," the green dragon informed her.

Aidyrth spread her wings and said, "This is a waste of valuable time. Get on my back."

"Wait! I said we had a deal," the Crow yelped.

"Free the were people. Now." Aidyrth punctuated her words with sheets of fiery ash.

The Crow uttered an odd, keening cry that made me wish I'd shut my ears. It was eerie and so riddled with evil, I'd spend the rest of my days trying to unhear it. The iron bars clattered to the ground. In one fluid movement, the crow flew level with the black dragon's forelegs and grabbed her head. Once she had it firmly between her talons, she shimmered into nothingness.

My people shambled forward. Cheering feebly, they stumbled toward me.

How could we move so many? Did they have a shred of power left amongst them?

The dragons had reverted to their language, the one where I caught one word in ten. Aidyrth bugled loudly. The crowd fell silent.

"I do not like what comes next, but it is necessary" she announced. "What you see, you will forget. Is that understood?"

"Aye," Alara replied. Most of the other werewolves echoed her assent.

"Good," the black dragon said. "For if you break your vow

and tell anyone not standing here about where we go and how we arrived there, your life will be forfeit."

An incredulous whine from my wolf mirrored my sentiments.

"Stand close," Aidyrth ordered. "As close to one another as you can. Do not fight our magic. It will not be comfortable, and there will be precious little air, but we must take you to a place we can heal your magic."

"Where is that?" Zeno asked. I've known him for centuries. He's an older were than I am with tawny hair, green eyes, and a lanky build.

The dragon shook her head. "No questions. Any who do not trust our intentions, move off to one side. Do it quickly, for we must be gone afore the Crow and her allies change their minds."

The air glowed, shifting through rainbow shades. Zeno took a step away from the others but sidled back. The prospect of being stuck here in his depleted state must have made him swallow his reservations.

"Where are we going?" my wolf asked quietly.

I didn't waste magic answering because I had no idea.

❧ 13 ❧

Aidyrth hadn't been kidding about not pleasant. A journey spell snapped up all of us. I marveled at the scope of its power. Unlike any travel spell I'd ever employed, this one included a rounded corridor four times the size of a usual spell.

Rather than standing still and waiting for our destination to appear, the dragons prodded us to walk as quickly as we could. It would have been simpler, but many of the werewolves could barely stand, let alone walk. I helped as many as I could, slinging an arm around them and dragging them along.

Soon, I was panting as the thin air took its toll.

I had questions, but the dragons were offended by anything that smacked of distrust. I'd find out where we were going soon enough.

Or not.

We trudged on and on and on wrapped in the dragons'

enchantment. My throat was raw from breathing smoke and thirst, but this transit had to be so much harder on my kinsmen. I'd had a chance to do a rough nosecount and came up with forty-four.

Not all of us, but damned close. We don't exactly have a central registry, and we should. If Anubis was going to wreak havoc on lives we'd constructed in his absence, we needed to keep track of who was where.

Was he the guiding light behind this? Odd he hadn't shown his snout today.

My lungs were on fire. No clothing to trap bits of air. I held the hand that wasn't gripping a female werewolf's shoulder over my mouth and nose, doing my damnedest to concentrate oxygen.

It helped a little.

"How did you know to look for us?" the werewolf next to me asked into my mind. Smart of her. Telepathy doesn't require oxygen, but it does require magic so hers couldn't be fully depleted.

"Ran into Alara in the dreamscape. Her insistence I accompany her felt off, so I returned home for reinforcements."

"Thank you for that." She stumbled, but I held on.

"Do you know why you were captured?"

She shook her head. Cropped blonde hair bobbed around her gaunt features. *"Nay. Not really."*

"But Anubis was part of it," I pressed.

A head nod.

"Did you actually see him?"

She stumbled again, almost hitting her knees on the bottom of the channel. I should leave her be. She'd been through enough. Still, the more information I had, the better prepared I'd be to deal with whatever happened next. If Anubis was masterminding this, he wasn't done.

I steadied her; we shambled on, our pace slowing by the minute. A quick glance around told me the other weres weren't faring much better. Those who were stronger aided others, but no one was moving at even a moderate pace.

The dragons had rearranged themselves. Aidyrth was in the lead, but the other two had taken up positions behind us, probably to ensure no one was left behind.

The heat in my lungs intensified; I struggled for every breath. If this continued much longer, none of us would reach the other end.

If there was one.

"You must walk." Aidyrth's voice reverberated off the channel walls. "I cannot create more air. We have passed the halfway mark, but, at your current rate of progress, 'twill be another hour or more afore we reach Fire Mountain."

Startled gasps morphed into coughing fits.

"This was the only way to move so many of you out of harm's way," she continued. "Our travel paths differ from yours. They consolidate magic and are far more direct. Unfortunately, they only lead to Fire Mountain. We have alerted our healers to be ready to receive you. Once you have been restored to health, you will be free to leave."

Behind me, a werewolf collapsed groaning.

"Get up!" the green dragon hustled forward and nudged him.

"Can't," he gasped and lost consciousness.

The dragon scooped him onto his back.

"Let them carry their own," Aidyrth instructed.

"Not sure they can," he bugled back.

What happened to those left in the dragons' travel paths? I wasn't sure I wanted to know. I had a feeling it wasn't pretty. Unlike the journey channels I was used to, this one pulsed with enchantment, almost as if it were sentient.

Perhaps it was.

Sentient and hungry for anything that might augment its magic.

The thought chilled me, almost as if I marched through the belly of an alien life form.

"Yessss," hissed into my mind.

It took me a moment to realize it had come from the were I was practically carrying. *"Yes, what?"* I probed.

"Anubis. I saw him."

"Are you certain? Have you ever laid eyes on him before?"

"Nay, but 'tis who he said he was. I had no reason to doubt him."

"Did anyone else express concerns?"

"Yes."

Her mind voice was a bare whisper. I gave my cavalcade of questions a rest. We had another hour to get through, but we had to keep moving. I picked up the pace, but my companion groaned so piteously I slowed again.

Pants and grunts came from all sides. The only ones not suffering were the dragons. Of course. I wished Aidyrth would have kicked this one around with me. Perhaps there'd been another way.

Like what? a sour inner voice asked. The dragons must have been desperate to allow so many into Fire Mountain, a spot reserved solely for them—and the odd prisoner like the Morrigan. If there'd been any other path, we'd be on it.

I needed to get over myself. Compared with my kin, I was

in tip-top shape after Aidyrth's infusion to shore up my reserves. It gave me an idea I was ashamed hadn't occurred to me sooner. Rather than blowing through magic urging the were clinging to me forward, far simpler to pass on Aidyrth's gift.

"Let me strengthen you," I suggested.

"How?" Her voice was bitter. In that moment, I recognized her. Gretta had changed so much, it made my heart ache. Once a proud daughter of our kind, she'd been reduced to a wizened crone. How had it happened so quickly? Surely the group hadn't been captive for more than a handful of weeks.

"Like this." I wriggled a psychic funnel into her magical center and pushed power her way. Not a lot. She couldn't tolerate much in her current state.

A weak smile painted her face. "Thanks, Grigori. You're the best." Her voice was back. Garbled and cracked, barely above a whisper, but back nonetheless.

"Ha. Self-serving as fuck," I growled. "Let's do this."

"Let's do this, indeed." She straightened, walking a little faster.

It was only an hour but one of the longest in my life. I've never known putting one foot in front of the other to take such concentration. And I had most of my resources. Gretta must be laboring, but she didn't complain.

"Ready yourselves," Aidyrth warned.

For what? Was this interminable journey almost over?

"There will be no air," she went on, "but then we'll arrive. Do not fight the sensation. It disrupts the energy channels. It's why we never, never bring those who aren't dragons—or prisoners—to Fire Mountain this way."

Her statement intimated I'd be capable of leaving there

on my own, using the travel pathways I was used to. Otherwise, how else were the lot of us going to return to Earth or wherever we chose to land?

The transition from scant air to none at all was instantaneous. After two or three panic-inducing non-breaths I covered my nose and mouth and quit trying to breathe. Aidyrth had said the next part would be over soon.

Except it dragged on and on. I grew lightheaded. My vision hazed over; I staggered. Before I went to my knees, I wove magic into a webbing I hoped would make up the difference.

Gretta had quit moving. She swayed on her feet. I returned to her and wrapped an arm around her waist, holding her upright as we floundered forward. Did we have to keep moving? My vision wasn't especially sharp any longer, but the world seemed to have stopped with weres sprawled on the floor of the channel. Some twitched. Others didn't move at all.

A lack of air shouldn't have such dire effects. Not this fast.

The dragons stood in a line in front of us bugling frantically. I'm far from a judge of such things, but they sounded as worried as I felt.

Why?

This was their territory. Their magic. Their portal.

Booming surrounded us, low at first but escalating in volume until my ears ached as much as my lungs. A thunderous crack was followed by a rush of superheated air. It was dry and burned the holy hell out of my mouth and throat, but I sucked it in anyway. Jolts of agony shot up my legs from my bare feet. I bounced from one to the other, but the stench of singed flesh made me gag.

Not only was the air hot; I stood on burning sand.

A strangled yelp from my wolf reinforced how painful the hot air was. His furry paws would have been better suited than naked flesh, but I wasn't ready to shift.

The channel had vanished replaced by an endless vista of scorching sand punctuated by a ring of mountains rising sharply in the background. The center mountain stood higher than the others, and it belched smoke.

"Fire Mountain, eh?" Gretta rasped by my side as she, too, picked up her feet to avoid the superheated surface.

I nodded. Pretty much had to be.

Aidyrth and the other two dragons turned to face us. "Some of you are traitors," she bugled. "We will discover who and make short work of them before you are allowed any further into our world."

My head snapped up. No wonder the Crow hadn't put up more of a fuss about releasing her prisoners. My second thought was Aidyrth must be mistaken. No werewolf would sell out to evil.

It's not in our natures.

"Not possible," Gretta panted, mirroring my impression.

"It was why we had such a hard time during the transit," the black dragon trumpeted. "None of us understood until toward the end when the air ran out. It told us everything since naught was left to hide behind."

Past caring if I drew attention to myself, I cupped my hands around my mouth and shouted, "Explain, please."

"We owe you nothing," Aidyrth snarled.

"You do not," I agreed. "If you're going to accuse my kinsmen of perfidy, I would know why."

"Save your breath, Grigori. I am guilty." Samael dragged

himself forward, limping badly. Dark hair hung around his face in tangles. His chest and back bore what might have been whip marks. Green eyes sunk into hollows in his gaunt face. Once strongly built, he'd turned into skin stretched over bones.

The black dragon shot fire at him, stopping shy of his feet. A visible truth net clanked over him. "Are you the only one?"

"Nay," a female voice rasped. Sierna, Samael's blood bonded mate, trudged to his side. Smoke rose from her feet, but she didn't appear to notice or care.

"Any others?" Aidyrth raked the group with her whirling gaze.

"Only us," Samael replied. He stood straight beneath her gaze but didn't look at her.

I pushed closer winding enchantment around my feet to preserve the flesh. "Why would you do such a thing?" I demanded. Confronted by proof of the dragons' assertion, I was furious.

"Does it matter?" Sierna shoved blonde hair behind her thin shoulders. "We sinned to save those we love."

The truth net was around Samael, but Sierna's words rang true.

"You weren't the only werewolves," I said flatly.

"Others remained in a different prison," she confirmed.

"What was the agreement?" Aidyrth aimed her question at Samael.

"We would leave the channel open so the Morrigan and Anubis could follow and snatch us back," he said dully. "In return, the other werewolves would be allowed out of their underground cells and given food."

"Did you tamper with our travel channel?" The green dragon arched a scaled brow.

"You already know the answer." Samael's voice cracked. "Dragon enchantment is far too powerful for werewolves to meddle with. We did try, though."

"It was the disturbance you felt," Sierna added.

I drew my brows together, confused. "But the Morrigan knew dragons rescued us. Surely, she knows the way to Fire Mountain since she was imprisoned here."

"The way is barred to her—and all others," the black dragon explained. "She will burn to a cinder if she attempts to cross the barriers protecting our world without one of us as an escort."

"Punish us as you see fit," Samael said wearily.

"No matter what you do, it won't be any worse than what we already lived through." Sierna leaned into him. Smoke rose from their feet; their breath was ragged.

"How long were you imprisoned?" I asked.

Samael shrugged. "Hard to say. Months. Maybe years."

It explained why they all looked so wasted.

The dragons had their heads together; hot dry air glistened around them as they communicated in their tongue.

Gretta gripped my arm silently urging me to intervene, but there wasn't anything for me to add. The dragons would extend mercy. Or not. This wasn't my world. I was a bit player here.

I motioned everyone close, creating a circle of slightly cooler sand for us to stand on. When Samael and Sierna hesitated, I dragged them closer saying, "No point burning your feet further."

"What difference does it make?" Samael grunted.

Before I could respond by telling him to pull his head out of his ass and stop feeling sorry for himself, the dragons turned as a unit and faced us. "We will proceed into the caves to preserve your skin from burning," Aidyrth said.

"You face a choice." The black dragon pointed at Samael and his mate.

"Choose wisely," the green dragon cautioned. "Last time, you did not."

My mouth opened. I swallowed my protest, my excuses, my statements about not thinking clearly when you've been whipped and starved. I'd have died before I let the Morrigan or Anubis force me into anything that brought shame on my head.

My people are proud, stiff necked to a fault.

"We will spare you," Aidyrth told them, "under the following conditions. You will subject yourselves to a thorough examination. During the process, we will search out any remaining connections between you and the Crow or Anubis. They will be expunged. It is possible some of your memories may be impacted along with them."

"If you refuse," the green dragon said, "your lives will be forfeit, and you will spend eternity in one of our fiery pits."

Samael and Sierna fell to their knees and bowed, touching their foreheads to the hot sand. "We accept your kind offer," Samael said.

"Aye, 'tis far more than we deserve," Sierna echoed.

"Get up." The green dragon's voice was gruff. "You will accompany me."

"And me," the black dragon bugled.

Without a word, the bonded pair rose and stumbled

across the hot sand. Given their depleted condition, they kept up with the dragons by sheer force of will.

"The rest of you follow me," Aidyrth instructed.

The second I stepped off the circle of cooler sand, my feet screamed in protest. Still, I lurched along. No one else was complaining, and they were in worse shape than I was.

"Do you know how many others remain with the Morrigan?" I asked Gretta.

"Twenty or so. They've been collecting us for years."

"We have to rescue them."

"How?" Her tone was laced with bitterness.

"I'll figure something out."

"You'll never find them."

"Not if I go hunting, but the Crow and Anubis are arrogant. They'll plan retribution for today. When they do, we'll be ready."

"I've always appreciated your optimism."

The dragon took a hard right and led us through a gash in the sand that had been invisible moments before. Relief was instantaneous. My lungs stopped protesting. My feet still ached; time and magic would heal them.

Sighs rose from all around me. Everyone had been suffering, but we're a tough lot.

Because I wasn't paying attention, I pitched into a line of werewolves ahead of me. When I looked up, two dragons had joined Aidyrth. "Everyone but Grigori will go with our healers. Once you are better, you will return to your homes."

I expected my kin to queue up and follow the new dragons. They did, but before leaving, everyone either hugged me or shook my hand.

Once they were gone, Aidyrth said, "You did a good turn

for them. Are you certain you still want to create a circle of assassins?"

"Of course I do. Why wouldn't I?"

Scales rattled. "You could be their leader if you wished."

I shook my head. "We don't operate that way. No royalty. No council structure. Every werewolf is created equal."

"Interesting." She puffed steam around me and beckoned with a talon. "Come. The others await us in one of the smaller chambers."

Others?

I considered asking, but I could wait. After a few twists and turns, we entered a cave. Quinn, Rhiana, and Delilah rushed forward. "There you are." Quinn slapped me across the shoulders.

I groaned as his palm hit burned skin.

"Where are Roland and Dorcha?" I peered through dim light seeking them.

"Right here." The unicorn trotted from a shadowed alcove with the eagle on her withers.

"This is as good a spot as any to map out our next moves," Aidyrth explained. "Far more private than any place on Earth or one of the borderworlds."

"All of you want to do this?" I glanced from one to the other. "Make the Circle a reality."

"We do," the dragon said firmly. "But we would understand if you chose to throw in your lot with your kinsmen."

"There is evil in the world far beyond the scope of simple castle assassins," Rhiana explained.

"We aim to address it all." Delilah smiled softly.

My gaze lingered on her in a question. She understood,

squared her shoulders, and faced me. "It was wrong to mislead the others about your intentions. I am content for you to lead us."

She held out a hand. I shook it.

"Did you develop an agenda?" I asked.

"A short one," Quinn said.

"Fill me in, and then I'm going to make a bid to squeeze rescuing the rest of the werewolves into our plans."

"We need to wait," Aidyrth cautioned.

"I said much the same to Gretta," I told her. "We can be hip deep in other projects, but when the Morrigan pokes her beak out—"

"We'll be ready," the dragon snarled. "Her cell awaits her. This time, she won't escape it."

"Meanwhile," Rhiana spoke up, "Dark Fae are cutting off access to borderworlds, and..."

Words swirled around me. I added to them here and there. We were gelling as a team; it felt right. Our time to pick up the banner had come. Expanding our horizons beyond accepting work from entitled monarchs added purpose to our endeavors.

"We still need a base of operations," I interrupted Quinn, who happened to be talking. "Even if we don't use it for that purpose, is everyone still up for taking Inverness Castle? James did promise it to me."

"We'll do that first," Dorcha whinnied.

"'Tis a most excellent location," Rhiana said. "Easy to protect."

"Wait a minute," I cut in. "Last time, Dorcha said it was too close to town."

"I rethought that." The unicorn tossed her mane.

"Aye, and while my place is isolated, it isn't really large enough," Aidyrth added.

"So, you do want to stake out Inverness as our first guild house?" I glanced around at nods.

"What are we waiting for?" Aidyrth trumpeted and wrapped us in dragon magic. Different from the last travel spell, this one tapped familiar channels. When it spit us out, we stood on the banks of the River Ness just past midnight on a cold, clear night.

The castle rose above us, a staunch presence splitting the night with its bulk.

A few of its high windows still sported light. The remainder were dark.

"We'll start on the upper floors," I said. "Quinn and I will sweep everyone down stairwells."

"The rest of us will meet them at the doors," Aidyrth said.

Dorcha whinnied. "Dragonfire and a unicorn's horn can be quite the inducement. Particularly if we make an example of anyone who doesn't leave quietly."

I rubbed my hands together. Good time to be a wolf, so I let the transformation take me.

"About time," my wolf grumbled.

"Forward. This will be exciting," I told him.

"Ready?" The dragon shot fire skyward, painting a castle wall.

"Never readier," I told her.

As a group, we surged forward.

14

Quinn and I scrambled up the uneven stonework, aiming for ramparts on the uppermost level. With a bit of a magical assist, the castle's walls offered sufficient hand, foot, and paw holds. Roland soared above us squawking encouragement. He wouldn't draw attention—unless anyone looked closely enough to be shocked by his size.

And his coloring. Bald eagles aren't native to this part of Scotland. White-tailed eagles and golden eagles are, and the white-tailed variety are every bit as large as normal bald eagles.

We had night on our side. Roland could caw up a storm, and no one would pay him the slightest heed, chalking him up as a night hawk of some type.

The parapet was deserted. I'd expected it to be. We ran along its length until we located a door into the castle proper. Quinn and I have worked together before. We didn't need words. He yanked open doors; I snarled and growled, chivvying sleepy lords and ladies from their beds.

Except this floor housed those of lower rank.

Shrieks and howls tore through the corridor as people ran this way and that wrapping robes over their sleeping attire. So far, this was entirely too easy, not like sport at all.

We moved one floor down employing the same strategy.

A lord flanked by three guardsmen met us in the center of the hall. One of the knights took a swipe at Quinn. He hit the blade with a shot of magic that melted it. Liquid metal pooled on the wooden floor creating a funnel of smoke. Before the whole place went up in flames—defeating our purpose—I sent magic of my own to quash the flames.

Four sets of fingers curved into the sigil against evil. The lord screeched like a scalded cat calling someone's name. The next door down the corridor banged open. A tall balding man sporting tattered black wizard's robes hurried to his side.

"Aye, mi'lord." The wizard's head bobbed on his stalk of a neck.

"Do something about them." The lord pointed at us.

Quinn focused on the newcomer and snorted laughter. "Best of luck, mate," he chortled.

A guardsman circled behind him, trying for stealth.

"I wouldn't try it." Quinn didn't bother turning around. "Unless you want to lose your weapon."

I rose up on my haunches, growling for effect. It worked. Everyone drew back, even the wizard who possessed about enough magic to maybe light a candle.

"You do not get to hide," the lord snarled at his minion. "Fix this."

"Trying my lord," the wizard mumbled. To his credit, his

voice didn't shake. His hands were raised in front of him directing a feeble thread of power, no doubt the best he was capable of.

Meanwhile the other occupants of this floor streamed around us, hustling down the stairwell. If there was a showdown, they didn't want any part of it. Roland chose that moment to fly through an open window at the far end of the hallway, his appearance unsettling enough to drive stragglers into double-time rhythm.

The wizard switched his focus to the eagle. Big mistake on his part. Roland dive bombed him, clipping off part of an ear. Blood flowed, coppery and viscous.

I wanted my voice, not the werewolf garbled version. *"It's just for a moment,"* I promised the wolf and flowed into my other form.

Faced with true power—with half his ear gone down the eagle's gullet—the wizard spun and pelted down the stairs following the rest of the crowd.

"You're fired," the lord shouted after him.

"I quit," floated back.

My transformation was complete. I stalked to the lord, ignoring his three henchmen. "You will leave," I ordered. "James promised this castle to me. He was supposed to clear it out. Since he failed in that endeavor, I'm forced to do it my way."

"You can't do that," the lord protested. "This castle belongs to me as it belonged to my forebearers. I am George Gordon, Fourth Earl of Huntley and the Sheriff of Inverness."

"Aye, and you serve at James's pleasure," I reminded him.

"He will set matters right," George mumbled.

"Don't count on it," I retorted. "Now, get moving and be

gone by daybreak. I'll allow you a few hours to collect your personal effects."

Quinn turned on me. "Why would you do that?"

"Because I'm kind. If it comes back to bite me, heads will roll."

My wolf grabbed the point; we shifted. He wasn't wrong. I'd said what I needed to. We padded down the hall with Quinn and Roland behind us. Footsteps pounded in our wake.

Really? George must be shy a few brain cells. Or he didn't give tuppence for his men. Maybe both. I leapt skyward, twisting in midair. Quinn turned as well, shouting, "The one on the right is mine."

I mowed into the other knight, closed my jaws around his throat, and ripped the vessels to shreds. Blood geysered everywhere, coating the walls and floor. Too bad. Maybe I'd make George clean up this ungodly mess, since it was his fault.

Quinn was neater than me. He grasped his opponent's neck, jerking it first to one side, then the other. The sound of cracking vertebrae was loud and satisfying. The third knight, the one absent a weapon, bent double and puked.

My wolf hooted laughter. What the hell kind of protector couldn't bear the sight of blood?

The color drained from George's face as he stared at the wreckage of his honor guard. Shame on him. He'd ordered them forward. No one to blame but himself for their untimely demise.

"Done yet?" Quinn asked in a casual tone after dropping the knight's lifeless body to the bloodstained floor.

Roland cawed merrily, fluttered to the ground, and

plucked an eyeball from the fallen knight, munching with enthusiasm. I'd forgotten how much he liked them.

George doubled up a fist and shook it my way. "James will hear of this."

"You bet he will." Quinn stole my thunder. "Because we're going to tell him. About that grace period. It just ran out. You will leave immediately."

I rubbed my bloody snout on his thigh. He snorted again. "This is the thanks I get? Bloody garments."

"Since when did you turn into such a prude?" I asked. *"We're assassins. Blood is where we live."*

"You'll notice my kill was neat, clean." He dusted his hands together. "Yours, on the other hand—"

I woofed to shut him up.

When I glanced at the hall, George was nowhere to be found. Apparently, he'd taken advantage of our lighthearted banter to make himself scarce. Good move on his part. He was beginning to annoy me.

"What the hell happened to you?" Rhiana burst into the upper hall. The clop of hooves on the stairs announced Dorcha's arrival.

The unicorn neighed loudly and drove her horn into the bloodiest of the two dead bodies. "We waited and waited for you," she whinnied.

"Aye, the castle is empty but for a few servants. Thought we might want to keep them around until we move in," Rhiana said.

"Eh, we had a bit of trouble with the laird. Seems he feels put upon," Quinn told her.

Dorcha pawed at the wooden floor making runnels in the

congealing blood. "He's gone too," she announced. "One of the last to leave. He freed all the horses on his way out."

Grateful Dorian hadn't been stabled there, I padded downstairs to take stock of our newly acquired property. Along the way, I nosed into this room and that. One of the bedchambers had a deep wardrobe. I shifted and grabbed breeks, a tunic, and a vest. All were a reasonable fit although the vest was a shred tight across my shoulder blades. No boots, but I don't mind going barefoot.

"Nice work tonight," I told the wolf.

"We didn't do much," he observed.

"But we could have if the castle's occupants hadn't been scared out of their wits. Besides, it's results that count. We accomplished what we set out to do."

"Can we go back and eat the one we killed? Roland ate the eyes, but there's lots left." The wolf sounded hopeful. And hungry.

"We could, but wouldn't you rather hunt? Human flesh is always tough and stringy."

Delilah and Aidyrth met me in the grand hall. Quinn, Rhiana, Dorcha, and Roland sauntered into the room.

"Now, can we get back to the list?" Aidyrth trumpeted.

"Of course," I told her. "I should pay James a visit in Edinburgh to let him know I'll be taking up residence here. It won't come as a surprise, and he'll need to find a new home for Georgie-boy and his people."

"Want reinforcements?" Aidyrth bugled. She sounded positively thrilled to flaunt her power.

"You'd certainly be the centerpiece of any conversation," I agreed. "But I need to do this on my own. I started it. He and I made a deal. He defaulted. I followed through. He must understand the same will happen any time he doesn't keep his word."

"You have another agenda," Delilah pointed out.

Had she always been prescient? "Aye. That I do. If we're going to make the Circle a success, we need every monarch throughout the region to funnel requests through me. So, my visit will lay out the process for him."

"What makes you think he'll accept anything from you after today?" Rhiana asked.

"He won't want to, but who's going to do his dirty work?" I countered. "While I'm at it, we should agree on a fair price for our work."

"Fifty gold pieces per kill," Rhiana shot back. "A hundred if we run into unexpected obstacles."

Quinn whistled and said, "Steep."

"We're worth it." Delilah dusted her hands together. "Enemies vanquished immediately. We'll be quick, clean, and anonymous. Who could ask for more?"

I'd originally thought to offer an introductory price, but why undercut the value of our skill?

"Fifty gold pieces it is," I agreed. "Will we barter the amount?"

"Depends," Quinn said. "If what's offered is something we need, we'll consider it."

I had what I needed. "I'm off," I told them. "If you leave, wrap the castle in warding, so no one can enter while we're away."

"I'll do you one better," Rhiana growled, sounding fierce. "I'll set things up so anyone crossing the lintel strangles. Not all at once, but a long, slow, painful ending." She paused.

"Those few servants I alluded to? They took off after their master."

"I love it," Delilah chimed in. "Won't take too many strangulations for mortals to decide the place is haunted."

"Word of mouth will be our ally," Quinn said cheerfully.

I laughed, did a bit of backslapping, and said, "I love all of you. Bloodthirsty bitches all around."

"That's us, all right," Dorcha whinnied.

After building a quick spell, I set out for Edinburgh. I'd get James out of bed, but I didn't care about his comfort. If he'd done his job properly, there'd have been no need to storm the citadel and take it by force. Not that much force had been needed.

I shook my head. Mortals had grown soft. Today's version was nothing like the hardy Vikings who'd braved the North Sea in longboats. Now those had been men.

I aimed for what used to be my quarters in Edinburgh castle. Muffled shrieks told me James hadn't lost a second farming out my room. Heedless of who I'd disturb, I fired a mage light and pushed the door open. It flickered on the naked breasts and buttocks of a well-endowed blonde lass, who'd jumped out of bed and was winding a sheet over her lush body. Closer inspection revealed one of James's many bastard sons in the bed. He took after his father dick-wise, the tiny appendage pointing at the ceiling.

For the lass's sake, I hoped he had good recuperative powers.

The man curled his lower lip. "What are you doing back here, Grigori? Da said you were gone for good."

Interesting. Perhaps James hadn't reassigned my quarters

after all, and the young couple had been in search of a trysting spot where they wouldn't be disturbed.

"Gone for good, eh?" I parroted back his words. "Is there a new castle assassin?"

"Da said we didn't need one."

Laughter spewed from me. I was still hooting with glee as I strode from the room leaving the horny youngsters to their bliss.

"What's he going to do when the vampires come back?" the wolf growled.

"Might not be our problem," I pointed out. *"Not if he's planning to go it alone."*

I hurtled down the stairs, taking them three and four at a time. When I hit the ground floor, my first stop was the throne room. It was empty, so I moved on to the royal bedchamber. Feminine laughter made me forgo knocking; I pushed the locked door open with magic.

Like father like son. Except in this instance, James had no less than half a dozen naked women reclining on his large bed. Sheesh. It was a wonder Scotland didn't fall apart. All the man did was rut.

I clapped my hands smartly. James's eyes snapped open. The woman who'd been fellating him froze mid-stroke.

"Leave," he thundered at me.

"Certainly. Of course," I agreed blandly. "Once I've said my piece. If you want an audience, I'm good with it."

Scotland's monarch blinked owlishly at the acres of female flesh, almost as if he'd forgotten all of them were present. His miniature penis, uncovered once the woman removed her mouth, was an exact replica of his spawn's.

"Say what you will and begone," he growled.

"Inverness Castle is mine—" I began.

James shot upright and stood opposite me. "You didn't."

"'Fraid I did. We had a deal. I made good on it."

"But what about George Gordon?"

I shrugged. "Who knows? He left on a horse as if hellhounds pursued him."

James narrowed his eyes. "Who helped you with this little endeavor?"

"A dragon, a unicorn, and—"

"Enough," he shouted and flapped a hand at me. "Leave. Now."

The ones who left were his harem. Apparently, they'd heard enough to disrupt their delicate sensibilities.

"Soon." I kept my tone soothing and chafed at coddling the old fucker. "There's a new project in the works. I've banded together with several other mages and their bond animals. If you want the type of service I used to provide for you, run it past me. One of my associates will ensure the job is done to your liking."

The king sneered. "And how much will that cost?"

"Less than it used to when you consider you're not longer providing food and boarding for me."

"That tells me less than naught."

"Fifty gold pieces per kill. More if we run into problems."

"Outrageous!" he shrilled. "I'll have the castle guard take care of things."

"Have it your way." I turned to leave, but then turned back. "Your guard will be adequate unless you face a magical enemy. Earlier tonight, George sacrificed two of his knights. He set them against us, and the results were predictable."

James normally pasty complexion turned a few shades

whiter. "Maybe if you leave, the vampires and other scum will too."

A corner of my mouth twisted downward. "Actually, quite the opposite. My presence has kept them at bay. You really do not want to alienate me. Wise monarchs don't burn bridges."

On that merry note, I strode from the room, patted a few asses as I sent the women back to entertain James, and considered where to go next.

Inverness Castle's stables were all but empty. I'd move Dorian and then join my fledgling Circle to pursue our first real assignment. Rhiana had bitched about Dark Fae blocking gateways. We'd set a few examples. Should send them scuttling for the exits. They're bullies at heart, and, like all bullies, they're cowards.

"Do you suppose we could take a short break and go hunting?" the wolf whined.

"Of course. We'll stop at the cottage to collect Dorian. You can hunt before we leave."

A growl filled my chest. Once the wolf's bloodlust was kindled, the only thing that satisfied it was more blood. I was hungry too, but excitement about the Circle of Assassins had eclipsed everything.

The group and our projects would still be there whenever we arrived. Keeping my other half happy edged to the top of my list.

"Wise move," the wolf observed. *"Very wise."*

"What were you going to do? Eat me?" I tugged power into an arc and ignited a journey spell.

The wolf didn't answer. He didn't have to. My question had been rhetorical, and both of us knew as much. Grateful for my dual nature and my longtime companion, I settled into the short wait between here and our destination.

Would Liliane be in the cottage? I hated to boot her out in the middle of the night, but the other option of allowing her to stay could be far worse. I wasn't attracted to her; she wasn't far removed from childhood.

But if her father tracked her and found the both of us in my cottage, I'd be stuck either killing him or wiping his memory.

"No good deed goes unpunished," the wolf noted with a merry yip.

"No one asked you," I replied sourly.

15

The moors spread before me as my spell dissipated. Night provided adequate cover, but I wound invisibility around me to be on the safe side. Not much in the way of trees to hide behind. Shepherds occasionally moved flocks at night—when they stole a sheep or two. Best if no one noticed my arrival. I took my bearings and snorted. Not especially accurate, my travel spell had spit us out half a league from the cottage.

I'd have gladly ceded forms were it not for wanting to hang onto the clothes I'd filched from Inverness Castle. The wolf pressed against our bond, angling for freedom, for his paws to eat up terrain and his fangs to sink into fat rabbits running this way and that.

"*Soon,*" I promised and received an unhappy growl in return.

We passed an occasional hut. All were deserted, which seemed odd to me, particularly the ones that hadn't fallen prey to the elements. Shelter isn't easy to come by. Shepherds are a hardy lot, but even they appreciate a break from Scotland's beastly weather.

The darkened hump of my cottage became visible in the distance. A mortal couldn't have seen it, but my night vision is excellent. I quickened my pace—until the fine hairs on the back of my neck quivered. At first I kept going, but a pervasive sense of wrongness bombarded me from all sides.

Something did not want me anywhere near the cottage.

Was I turning into a doddering old woman afraid of my own shadow? Magical senses on full alert, I searched the darkness for clues.

A shrill whinny was followed by several more. Hoofbeats pounded across wet earth, making squelching sounds as my horse pelted by dragging a lead rope. Had he chewed through it?

I pushed into his mind. Horsey images spilled through me. The stallion was terrified. If his version was to be believed—and it was farfetched as hell—demons had converged on the cottage and were painting everything with blood. For a time, it had been his blood before he'd knocked one senseless with his powerful hind legs and chewed through another's arm.

No longer running, I crept through darkness until only about fifty meters separated me from the cottage. Whoops and squeals were tough to interpret—until I heard a low, traumatized whine.

Liliane.

As if she didn't have enough on her plate.

"How many do we face?" I asked the wolf. Even when he's not primary, he's still better at determining that type of thing.

"Five. No, make that six. We could use a spot of help."

"By the time they get here, Liliane could be dead."

"She's not far from it now."

I trusted his judgement. We had to do something; waiting for support was a luxury. Raising my mind voice, I called Aidyrth and Dorcha. They'd be more likely to hear me over distance. And then I added Roland to the mix.

I hustled out of my clothes, securing them under a largish rock and let the transformation take me. Once we were fur and fangs, we raced toward the cottage and leapt through the open window. Glass is only for the gentry. Humble folk cover openings with cloth.

Or not at all.

We landed on all fours. The wolf dug in his claws to avoid slipping in a sea of equine blood. No wonder Dorian bolted. The place reeked of his blood—and his fury. The other end of the rope he'd been tied with dangled from a stake driven into the dirt floor.

The wolf had been right about six demons, but only four were still on their feet. One was unconscious, another crouched in a corner reassembling a severed arm. Tall, red, and scaly, they sported horns, hoofs, and barbed tails. Obscenely large genitalia brushed the ground.

My appearance dragged their attention from Liliane. She lay on her side huddled in a pool of blood, mostly hers but some belonging to Dorian. Her eyes were shut, her breathing a shallow pant.

The demons formed a line between me and her. Teeth bared, they hissed. One lunged for me. The wolf evaded him easily.

Four against one are shit odds. If we attacked, the

remaining demons would pile onto our back. Still, we had to do something. The wolf is better at brute force; I'm more skilled wielding magic.

Magic.

I had a temporary answer. I'd teleport Liliane out of here —and hope she didn't bleed to death before I got to her. For it to work, I needed to be next to her, which meant on the other side of the demon line.

"Begone," one snarled, showing a mouthful of rotten teeth.

I snarled back, grateful they weren't mobbing me but suspicious about their motives. They could jump on me—all four of them. Why weren't they?

"They must be waiting for someone," my wolf observed and feinted sideways to avoid a curved talon.

"We are too," I retorted.

Hanging about anticipating rescue—or annihilation if one of Hell's princes was on the way—isn't my style. And it sure wasn't doing Liliane any good. Her face was growing whiter by the moment.

"Work your way to her," I instructed and tugged a ragged spell together. My timing would have to be spot on. The spell had to be ready to go the second we crouched over her inert form.

The wolf didn't question me. He never does in dicey circumstances. With no warning, he leapt straight up. Clearing the demons by the smallest of margins, we landed with our paws surrounding Liliane.

I launched my spell, and she vanished.

Excellent. One task down.

The demons bellowed anger. I'd snatched a choice morsel from under their noses. They'd get even with me.

Fury rained down on us. The demons were done with our cat-and-mouse game. They attacked in synchrony, raining blows on my furry hide. The wolf closed his jaws around a throat, ripping through arteries and veins. If the hut had been bloody before, it paled in comparison to its current state.

Stinking black demon ichor spewed every which way. Talons and teeth scratched, bit, and tore as the other demons took advantage of the wolf's jaws being occupied. Pain seared me. Blood oozed from a dozen places. I directed healing magic to our hurt spots to buy us time.

Should I teleport us out of here?

I tested a few threads of magic. They bounced back and slapped me. Our enemy hadn't expected me to move Liliane; they'd taken steps to ensure I couldn't run the table with that trick again.

The hut door slammed open. I couldn't take my attention from the demons who wanted me dead, but I spied the stable lad from the corner of one eye. Too bad I couldn't talk with him. I'd have told him to find his sister.

The wolf barked a sharp warning. Some languages are universal. The lad turned and bolted into the night. He was resourceful. Hopefully, he'd find Liliane. I hadn't moved her far.

Magic and mortals aren't a good combination. The less exposure she had to enchantment, the better. It's addictive until all the mortal can think about is more of the same. Some refuse food and drink until death takes them.

Something sharp sliced down my rear leg. I pushed magic to stem the worst of the injury. The wolf was doing his best.

He'd released the first demon, but the others were wise to his strategy and twirled out of his reach.

Blood dripped from his jaws and from dozens of hurt places. The rancid reek of poison alerted me our time was running out. I've fought demons before. Some of them are like snakes with venom pouches pumping toxins through their fangs and talons.

How much magic did we have left? Not as much as I'd have liked.

The effects of the poison were insidious. We were weakening, not quickly, but a slow sinister tide was washing away our ability.

"We have to get out of here," I said.

"How? You checked, and teleporting is out."

"The old-fashioned way by running out the door."

"Not my style," he growled.

"Not mine, either, but they poisoned us. If we remain, our freedom is forfeit."

The wolf's silence told me he hadn't noticed.

We wove this way and that. Suddenly, we had a straight shot at the still-open doorway.

Would we grasp the opportunity—probably our only one —or would pride win the day?

Whichever of us is in ascendence makes those kinds of decisions. I'd already pitched my preference. I'm no coward, but living to fight another day is high on my list. The wolf feinted left, and then right. He snapped at a scaled hamstring. When the demon reacted by twisting away, we shot through the door.

We hadn't made it a hundred meters before the distinctive sound of dragon bugles turned us around. Quinn and Rhiana burst through a glowing portal along with their bond animals. Aidyrth and Delilah swooped low, thudding to earth next to the cottage.

The dragon aimed fire through the doorway.

Demons streamed outside, arms raised and black lightning forking from outstretched hands. Dorcha squealed outrage and plunged her horn into one demon breast after another. They fell in their tracks.

Unicorns are the executioners of the magical world. They're the only creature who can deal certain death to other immortals.

We reached the group when the last demon fell. The effects of the poison were stronger now. My head felt fuzzy, and our gait wasn't steady. Before I couldn't, I forced a shift.

"Two more in the hut," I gasped. Dorcha ran through the door, intent on ending them too.

"What happened to you?" Delilah ran to my side.

"Demon poison," Rhiana answered for me.

"It'll wear off," I mumbled and pitched to my knees, swaying like a drunk. Before I passed out, I said, "Find Liliane. I teleported her out of there."

Delilah knelt next to me. "Who is she?"

"Tavern wench. Hard times. Needed place to stay." My words were slurring. Remaining on my knees was hard. I wanted to close my eyes and go to sleep.

"I'll look for her," Delilah reassured me.

Rhiana joined us. Or maybe she only joined me, and Delilah had already left. Or perhaps she'd been there all along. My usually sharp mind had taken a hike. She gripped my forearm hard. "Fight it, Grigori. If you give in to this, it will take a pisspot of magic to bring you back."

"Trying," I mumbled.

Power flowed into me from where her fingers circled my arm. Bright, glowing, healing. I soaked up the offering like nectar. My head quit spinning; my vision cleared. I hadn't realized how fractured it was.

The small group, minus Delilah, gathered around me. Dorian had returned at some point and nuzzled me with his snout. I'd have laughed if I weren't so depleted. He'd never been overly fond of me, but, compared with demonspawn, I must have looked like a savior.

"Why were demons here?" Aidyrth bugled.

"Aye, we'd all like to know," Quinn said.

"They were here when I arrived," I explained. First, they were using Dorian's blood for something. When he bolted, they switched to Liliane."

"Found her," Delilah called from somewhere off to my left. Moments later, she staggered toward us with the unconscious girl in her arms. "I did some healing. She'll make it."

Breath swooshed from me. Thank all the gods and goddesses.

"Hold up." Rhiana let go of me and glided toward the cottage. "I want a closer look at this spell they were crafting."

I pushed upright, shivering. While Rhiana gathered data, I trudged to where I'd left my clothes, dressed, and returned to everyone.

Liliane was sitting holding her head in her hands. "What happened?" Her voice quavered. "Who are all these people?"

"I cleared her memories," Delilah said into my mind.

"You're safe. It's all that matters. But you need to return home. What's your brother's name?"

"Why?"

"He came by looking for you."

"Jonas. His name is Jonas."

"Call him," Delilah suggested. When Liliane complied, Delilah augmented her words with tracking enchantment.

He must have been close because he appeared almost instantly and crouched next to his sister. "Are you all right?"

"Not sure."

"Take her home," I told him.

Jonas glanced at me over a shoulder. "Canna. Da's drunk again."

"Take Dorian. Ride for Inverness Castle. When you get there, put the horse in the stable with feed and water. Find your way to the servants' quarters and get some rest."

Jonas's eyes widened. "But the laird willna allow it."

"I am laird there now. Go."

He helped Liliane to her feet and then onto Dorian. Once she was secure, he hopped up behind her and clucked to the stallion to walk on.

"Are you planning on having them stay?" Quinn asked.

I shrugged. "Maybe. We could use a servant or two. Hard to say."

"They're not important," Rhiana cut in. "I cast a few runes. The demons were here for you. Had they finished their blood casting, it would have crushed you the second you crossed beneath the lintel."

"They couldn't kill me," I protested.

"Nay, but they could knock you out and cart you off to goddess only knows where." She paused to spit in the dirt. "Who would have done this?"

I didn't have to search too deep. "James is the only one

who knows I frequent this cottage." Breath rattled from my lungs. "A bigger question is how he learned to parley with demonspawn."

"Does it matter?" Delilah arched a fair brow.

"Not at all," Quinn replied. "What does is ensuring his harassment stops here."

"Easier said than done," I muttered.

Delilah spun one hand in a get-on-with-it gesture. I nodded. "We can't murder the king of Scotland. If we do, none of the monarchs will send work our way."

"We could be sneaky about it." Rhiana tapped a foot.

Aidyrth shot fire into the sky. "Indeed we could. No one would ever know."

"You wouldn't need to be involved." Quinn grinned, clearly embracing the idea.

I held up a hand. "Whoa. Slow down, everyone. I'm not sure we need to scrub James."

"If not him, then whom?" Rhiana asked.

"I'm far more interested in how he forged an alliance with Satan, or his princes. Did he do it through his vampire connections?" I paused to consider the ramifications. "Once we know who's running the show, we punch a hole in their activity—"

"And scare James out of his boots," my wolf put in.

"Did you all hear that?" I glanced around at nods.

"James is a coward," I went on. "Making him believe we'll torment him like hellhounds shouldn't be difficult, particularly not if we make hash out of his wicked pets."

"I still say we're better off with him dead," Quinn said flatly.

"It may come to that," I agreed. "But if we don't sever his

connection with wickedness, they'll just seduce whoever takes his place. And we'll have the same problem all over again."

"Let's return to the castle," Rhiana suggested. "We can rest and eat and firm up our next steps."

"What will you do about the children?" Delilah asked me.

"Liliane and her brother?" At her nod, I went on. "I'll talk with them. If they remain, they're bound to overhear us on occasion. They must be sworn to absolute secrecy."

"It will never work," Delilah said.

"It could." I contradicted her. "I won't know until I sit down with them."

"For now, we must construct sound shields around all discussions," Rhiana cautioned.

I snorted. "No sound shield in this world—or any other— will hide a dragon and a unicorn from view."

"They're already seen us," Dorcha whinnied.

"Part of my conversation will be a mind sweep to see if they've talked with anyone," I reassured her. "Although I don't see how they could have since they traveled from here to the castle. My bet is they're both sound asleep."

"They're mortals," the unicorn went on. "Why are they so important to you?"

Her question caught me by surprise. I mulled it over. When I came up with an answer, it surprised me. "There's little enough good in the world," I said slowly. "The reason we eradicate evil is to ensure it doesn't spread its tentacles over everything, wiping out the light. Those children are innocent. If I have my way, they'll remain so."

"You can't save everyone," Delilah said softly.

"Since when is that a reason to turn my back?" I

countered, followed by, "Come on. Dawn will be here soon, and I would be gone from this place."

"What about the blood?" Rhiana jerked her chin in the direction of my hut.

"I'll meet the rest of you in Inverness," I told her. "This cottage isn't usable anymore, not by me, anyway. Demonkind know its location. I'll bundle my possessions and bring them to the castle. Once I've cleared everything out, I'll set a cleaning spell to knock out the worst of the carnage. That way someone will be able to use the hut. They'll be safe enough without me here."

"Are you certain?" Quinn arched a dark brow.

Was I? Demons had waltzed in and terrorized Dorian and Liliane.

"No, but shelter is precious. Our only other option is tearing this hut to the ground, and I'm not willing to do that with winter nearly upon us."

"Softhearted for an assassin," Rhiana muttered.

I flashed her a smile. "You are too. I've seen you coddle street urchins at those shows where you and Dorcha perform."

"Fair enough." She extended a hand. I grasped it and then did the same around the circle.

My friends. My allies. My brand-new partners in the assassin trade.

16

My proposal must have satisfied everyone. They walked through a gateway, leaving me alone on the moors. I worked quickly bundling the few possessions I'd relocated from Edinburgh Castle. I could have sent them to Inverness alone, but it was safer to travel with them. The in-between place is strange. Others with magic can break into travel spells, subverting them. Not that I was expecting sabotage, but, after today, I needed to keep my guard up.

I'd underestimated James. I'd not make that error again.

Two trips later, I was back in the hut. Dawn was breaking, turning the eastern skyline a deep purple. A few words activated a clearing spell. It would cleanse the worst of the mess and purify the place of wickedness, so it wouldn't serve as a beacon for monsters to converge.

James might have it in for me, but it wasn't a reason to put everyone who lived on this moor in danger. As I'd packaged and transported, I'd grown more and more angry. I'd done naught but good for him, and this was my payment?

How dare he?

"I like Quinn's idea about killing him," the wolf piped up.

"Leaning that direction myself. You never did get to hunt. Would you like to before we leave here?"

Pressure against our bond told me he loved the idea. Once again, I stashed my clothes and sat back while he caught jackrabbits, a vole, and a raccoon. When our gut was comfortably distended, we entered the hut and shifted again.

I dressed and set a spell to take us to our new home in Inverness Castle.

My first stop was the stable to check on Dorian. He dozed contentedly in a nice, safe stall with hay and oats in the feed hopper. I scanned his body for injuries, but someone had gotten to him first and healed the deepest of his cuts. Places demons had chopped through flesh to encourage blood to flow.

I still had no idea what type of blood spell the monsters were crafting and made a note to ask Rhiana since she'd identified it immediately. After leaving the horse, I strolled through the empty courtyard. What a difference from when George Gordon had occupied this place.

Then the castle had bustled with activity. I rather preferred it this way.

The fledgling Circle of Assassins sat around a rectangular table in one of the kitchens eating some type of stew with fresh bread. I slid into a seat, filled a bowl, and broke off a hunk of bread.

"We should enjoy this," I said before settling in to eat. It had probably come from the kitchens and been the product of departed scullery staff.

"We could hire a cook," Quinn ventured.

"Like hell," Rhiana retorted.

Aidyrth took up one corner of the room, Dorcha the other. Roland perched on the table, dipping his beak into the stew from time to time.

"How are the children?" I asked between bites. Was there any mead in the cellars? If not, there had to be spirits of some kind.

"Like you predicted, dead to the world," Delilah replied. "I scanned their minds. So far, so good."

"But they've been here all along," I protested. "How could it be otherwise?"

"The girl was in the cottage with them," Rhiana pointed out.

"Aye," Delilah chimed in. "Had to make certain she hadn't forged an alliance with them beforehand."

It never occurred to me; I chided myself for being too trusting and buried my discomfiture in a few more bites. I wasn't especially hungry. We'd just hunted, but meals serve many functions. In this instance, it was a venue for solidifying our brotherhood.

"Before you got here, we were discussing James," the dragon said. For once, she managed to not punctuate her words with flames. Good thing. A whole lot of Inverness Castle is wooden. Its timbers would go up like a torch.

I sopped bread into the stew. "And?"

"We still think he's expendable," Delilah answered.

"Aye," Rhiana went on. "The queen just gave birth to a girl child. They named her Mary Stewart. The line of succession is assured, but it will be years afore the child takes up the banner of leadership."

"Meanwhile," Quinn cut in, "the kingdom will be managed by court nobles vying for power. Once we get James out of the way."

I snorted. "I'll lay you odds the babe meets with an unfortunate accident and never becomes queen."

Rhiana shook her head. Dark hair wafted around her head. "I've scryed this. The babe will come into power, but she'll be forced off the throne years into her reign. That part isn't important."

"What is"—Quinn picked up the tale—"is the current battle. Scotland invaded England a month or so ago. It isn't going well."

First I'd heard of it, but then I rarely pay attention to mortals' wars. "James isn't there," I said, followed by, "Damn the man. The least he could do is show up for his troops."

"True enough. He left Edinburgh a few hours ago for Falkland Palace in Fife," Quinn said.

I snorted laughter. "Guess he didn't want another run in with me. How do you know where he went?"

Quinn shrugged his broad shoulders. "Know your enemy, mate. Cuts down on surprises."

"Most of his personal guard is in Solway Moss with the rest of his forces," Delilah added.

I held up a hand. "Let me guess. We're following him closely because we're planning to poison him."

"Not we," Dorcha whinnied. "You. We assumed you'd want him to know you were the instrument of his demise."

"*I like it,*" the wolf said.

I wasn't certain I did. "What makes you think he'll eat or drink anything from my hands?"

"He probably wouldn't," Delilah agreed. "Which is why you'll ward yourself, taint something you're certain he can't resist—"

"Spirits," I cut in.

"Spirits it is." Delilah grinned.

"So, I sneak in, add nightshade—or something equally deadly—to the flagon near his bed, and stand back and wait until he begins foaming at the mouth?"

"Something like that." Quinn nodded.

"I may not be able to reveal myself to him," I cautioned the others. "Once he hits a downward spiral, he'll be surrounded by physicians and courtiers."

"But him knowing it was you is the best part," Aidyrth protested.

"Not if they clap him in irons," Delilah contradicted her bondmate.

"I'll play it by ear," I said. "Hang on. All this talk of spirits is making me thirsty."

On my feet, I headed for a stairwell leading downward. The castle's lower level contained dungeons—and a spacious wine cellar. From the looks of it, we wouldn't run out of drink for a very long while.

I snapped up a bottle of mead and another of brandy before joining the others. "James has a taster," I muttered. "I pushed him into it."

"Means you'll need to time your infusion," Rhiana said.

"Aye," Quinn agreed. "After the taster and before James polishes it off."

"We'll be close," Aidyrth assured me. "In case something goes wrong and you require assistance."

I bristled. "Naught will go wrong. You can work on your next project, whatever you decide is most critical."

Delilah reached across the table and placed a hand over mine. "We're all used to working alone. It's the biggest challenge we face forming your guild: getting past our aversion to joining forces."

My cheeks heated. She'd nailed me dead to rights. "Be glad to have your company," I choked out and opened the bottle of mead. Not bothering with a mug, I tilted the bottle to my mouth and drank deeply.

Once I was done, I passed it to Quinn, who sat next to me.

"We're decided then." I glanced around the group.

"We are," Dorcha whinnied.

"Then we should get on with things," I said. "We leave at dusk."

I stood. "I'm going to talk with the children. Would anyone object if they're willing to remain here and serve us?"

After a pause where things could have gone either way, no one opposed the idea. "We haven't seen the last of George Gordon," I noted.

"We assumed the same," Quinn said.

"We're finetuning a spell to scare the daylights out of any human stupid enough to approach the castle," Rhiana murmured.

"Aye, it's nearly ready," Quinn added.

I arched my brows into question marks. She went on, "None of our magic will impact Liliane or Jonas—unless they cross beneath the outer wall."

Good to know. I'd weave it into my discussion with them.

Determined to either include them or scrub their minds of any memory of us, I walked up several flights of stairs to the servants' quarters and let myself into the tiny room where Liliane and her brother shared a narrow bed.

I assumed they slept this way at home. Bedding was a luxury, but they could each have their own room if they wished it.

Reaching into their minds, I brought them back to consciousness. Liliane jolted awake. Jonas groaned and rolled over before his sister jabbed him in the ribs.

"'Tis the laird. Look smart." She rocked from foot to foot and dragged her brother upright beside her.

"How are you feeling?" I asked her.

"Better than earlier." She offered a wan smile.

"Excellent. Apologies. If I'd had any idea offering my cottage put you in line for an attack by supernaturals, I'd never have done it."

Her eyes widened. "Were those really, uh, what they looked like?"

"Aye. Demonkind."

A shudder racked her slender frame, followed by several more.

"Would you like me to alter your memories?" I asked.

She shook her head. "Best if I remember. I know what they look and smell like. Maybe next time, I can run."

"You'll never outrun them, lass." I turned my attention to Jonas. "You did a good job with Dorian. Thank you for stabling him and seeing he had feed."

He hung his head, gaze glued to the floor. Having met

their father, my bet was no one cut these two any slack. If they didn't work from dawn till dusk, the whip came out.

"I have a proposition for you," I began.

Liliane looked at me. Jonas continued to stare at the floorboards.

"We will require assistance with day-to-day operations in the castle. All the servants left along with George Gordon and his retinue."

"But there's only two of us," Liliane mumbled.

"Aye, well there's not many of us, and the dragon and unicorn and eagle don't require anything. What we had in mind was cooking and caring for Dorian and any other draft animals we bring here."

"There must be a catch," Liliane said.

I smiled. "Bright girl. There is, and it's a big one. You will not be able to leave here. You will vanish from village life. People will assume you were killed by robbers or wild animals."

"So, we'd be prisoners?" Jonas found his voice.

"In a sense," I agreed. "In another, you'd have a far better life here than in your father's common house. You'll have comfortable beds, sufficient food, and long hours with naught to do."

"Except we canna leave," Liliane said. At my nod, she went on, "If we refuse?"

"You may go in peace, but me or one of the other mages will alter your memories so you cannot tell anyone about us."

"What if we promise to be silent?" Jonas asked.

"You'd mean well," I told him. "Promises like that have a way of getting away from you. A wee bit too much drink, or a wife or close friend who swears they'll never tell... Surely, you can see the problem."

"If we leave, will we ever be able to return?" Liliane asked.

I shook my head. "If you leave, you will forget everything that transpired from the night you saw me shift forms."

"Can we talk about it?" Liliane asked me.

"You have an hour," I replied and walked out of the room.

While the children were debating their future, I returned to the others.

"Here." Rhiana handed me a vial.

"What's in it?" I asked.

"A special mixture that's all my own." She smiled with a lot of teeth. "No telltale taste to give it away. Works very fast. Takes very little."

I tested the seal to make certain it wouldn't leak and tucked it into an inner pocket. "Thank you."

"We've been nagging her for the recipe," Delilah said.

"So far, no dice." Quinn made a sour face.

Eventually, years down the road, this castle would have a library far different from its current one. A collection of books and scrolls to augment our magical practices. Now wasn't the time to mention it, but once we trusted one another more, we'd pool our resources and be stronger because of it.

"What did the children say?" Dorcha whinnied.

"They requested time to decide."

The unicorn tossed her head. Power flowed from her, snaking upward. "Whew." She made a nickering noise. "For a moment there, I was worried they'd decided to sneak out of here."

For the second time, an alternative that had never

occurred to me slapped me in the face. "Their time is almost up," I said and headed back upstairs.

They sat on the edge of the bed, but scrambled to their feet when they saw me. Both youngsters bowed low.

"We want to stay," Liliane said.

"Da will come looking for us," Jonas mumbled. "We're the only help he has."

"He'll never get in here," I reassured them. "For the same reason you can't leave, no one can get inside without our permission."

"Are you certain?" the boy asked. "He'll be powerful mad."

"Quite. Your first jobs will be to take stock of foodstuffs. Do the best you can to preserve the perishables. Make certain Dorian is fed."

"How can I exercise him if we canna leave?" Jonas asked.

It was a good question. The lad clearly knew something about horses. "Ride him around the courtyard. After I'm back, I'll come up with a more permanent solution."

"Where are you—? Liliane clapped a hand over her mouth. "Apologies, my laird."

"None required. Another task for you is to cull through whatever clothing the servants left. Find a few items that fit you. If any alterations are required, I assume one of you can sew."

"We both can," they said in unison.

Before I left, I skimmed their minds to ensure they'd told me the truth without any subterfuge. They passed my test.

Pleased I'd chosen well, I turned and trotted down the stairs. A couple of hours remained before the time we'd selected to leave. The room where we'd shared a meal was empty. Rather than hunt the others down, I wandered through the castle choosing a modest set of rooms for my own. Once it was done, I moved the possessions I'd transported from the hut into them.

My dream, the Circle of Assassins, was coming together. After crossing the room, I laid my hands on the windowsill and stared out at the walled courtyard and beyond. My rooms were high enough to see over the wall. So far, the goddess had been with me.

She didn't desert me now. At the very edge of my distance vision, troops mustered. George Gordon hadn't lost any time, particularly since most of the Scottish forces were supposed to be in Solway Moss. The idiot was going to take a stand to get his castle back. And James, bastard turncoat, must have diverted some of his forces. How unpatriotic of him.

"He's still in league with demonkind," the wolf snarled.

I slapped my forehead with a palm. Of course. Solway was leagues to the south. The only way troops could have made it here this quickly was with a magical assist.

Pfft. We'd see how far George's gambit got him.

"Aidyrth."

"Aye."

"If you're not busy, could you fly to the east. Soldiers gather."

Dragon laughter rolled through me. *"Perfect place for fire. I'll lay down a line betwixt them and us."*

"I heard that," Dorcha broke in. *"I'll roust the unicorns. Between us and fire, bet they give up damned fast."*

"I want in on the fun," the wolf growled.

"Me too, but we're not alone anymore," I reminded him. *"Let's wait and see if they need us."*

I kept my eyes trained on the horizon. Aidyrth's form blocked out the westering sun. Fire rained from her open jaws. My sensitive ears picked up the clop of many sets of hoofs.

Unicorns swept into view. Hazy behind the growing tower of fire, they jabbed this way and that with their horns. Needing to be part of the battle won out; I stripped, and the wolf took over.

Not bothering with stairs, he leapt out the open window and hit the ground with all four paws churning up dirt. The main gateway in the wall circling the castle stood open. We raced through it. Excitement caught me up. We'd kill something before this was over; I'd make certain of it. Many somethings.

"Of course we will," the wolf announced. *"We're assassins. It's where we live."*

I'd have told him I loved him, but it would have made him squirm. Instead, I focused on joining the battle and squashing George Gordon into the ground. I'd be damned if I'd watch my back for the next twenty years until he had the good grace to die.

Nay. Today, we'd finish this. My wolf salivated at the prospect and ran faster.

17

I tugged magic around us so we could cross Aidyrth's fire. Dragonfire burns in perpetuity even absent fuel. Screams, howls, and groans joined the clank of armor. Demons—or someone—had transported a surprising number of men given Scotland's other battle, the one on Solway Moss.

Was anyone even left at the outpost in Northern England? Did James give a bloody fuck so long as he eviscerated me? What a fool.

I reached to pat the vial of poison with his name on it but remembered it was in the pile of clothing I'd left in my rooms.

While I was ruminating and building a case to end James's pathetic excuse for a life, the wolf began mowing through men. Between Aidyrth flying overhead spewing fiery ash, and six unicorns tromping through the field, George's men were terrified.

Many turned their horses, intent on escape, but George

sat dead center behind them with a line of knights fanned out on either side. Whenever a soldier made a break for it, one of the knights took off after him.

Blood soaked into the ground. The air reeked with its bright, coppery taint. Spilled entrails mingled with it, creating a spicy mélange only found on battlefields. Arrows nicked us, but the warding I'd crafted to move us through the fire unscathed was enough to deflect them.

The wolf tossed another body aside. Blood streamed down our jaws, coating our muzzle and chest. He lifted his nose, scenting the air. It wasn't like him to quit midstream, so I checked along with him.

"More demons," the wolf howled.

Made sense since something magical had to be behind all these armored men and their steeds appearing out of nowhere. I'd already figured that part out even absent the wolf's observation.

Raising my mind voice, I alerted my companions.

"Already see them," Aidyrth bugled, not bothering with telepathy. She turned her fire toward the north. Unicorns galloped the same direction.

We vaulted through the air, knocking a solider off his mount. The wolf pinned him to the ground. *"Wait,"* I told him. *"We need information."*

"What makes you think he knows anything?" The wolf opened his jaws, positioning them around the hapless man's neck. To his credit, he didn't beg for his life.

"Let's find out," I said and forced a shift.

The man's eyes grew big as pinwheels, with white showing all around the iris. His breath came in shallow, panting gasps, but he still didn't plead for mercy.

"Who is behind this?" I demanded. Like the wolf, I crouched over the man, holding him down with hands on his shoulders and knees on his thighs.

"Don't know," he gritted.

I curved one hand around his neck and pressed on his windpipe. "Try again," I urged.

"The earl wants his castle back." He swallowed convulsively.

"Aye, I get that part. But you're not one of his men. You're wearing the king's colors." It was a shot in the dark on my part. If James's court had colors, I'd never noticed before.

The man blinked once, and then again. The battle raged around us. Unicorns were probably kicking demon asses, judging from the pleased trumpets issuing from Aidyrth.

I pressed harder on his neck. "Last chance, mate."

"You're going to kill me anyway," he growled in a show of spirit considering his circumstances.

"Maybe not."

"Even if you don't, the earl won't let us leave." A shudder racked him. "None of us knew there'd be demons and suchlike."

I just bet they didn't. Would have put a real damper on recruits.

"Are you part of James's retinue?" I asked pointblank. "Answer truthfully. I'll know if you don't." Within me, the wolf was restless. He wanted to get back to killing, and I was standing in his way.

I allowed him to form a shadow behind me to hurry things along.

"What are you?" The soldier's eyes grew wider still.

"Does it matter?" More pressure on his neck until his chest strained for breath.

Finally, he nodded. "Aye, most of us were on Solway Moss. A black rider bearing James's seal diverted us. Promised this would be quick and then we'd return to Solway. After we agreed, demons showed up. We tried to run away, but—"

It was all the answer I needed. I moved off him. "You're free to go."

He laughed bitterly. "Would it were true."

I stood and took stock. The bulk of the battle had moved a couple of hundred meters to the north. "If you get on your horse and ride toward the castle, you'll end up in the village. No one will stop you."

He didn't wait around for me to change my mind. On his mount as quickly as a man in full armor can manage—which isn't all that fast—he turned and urged his horse to a gallop.

As I'd predicted, no one gave chase.

The wolf was already halfway there. I stepped back and ceded to him. A quick jaunt led to a circle of dead demons with unicorns neighing victoriously. The only soldiers left standing were George Gordon's knights with him dead center in their midst.

There weren't enough dead to account for the rest of his force, so many must have taken advantage of the demons' arrival to get the hell out of here.

George waved a dirty white handkerchief, no doubt a sign of surrender. I wasn't in the mood to shift yet again, so I trotted to Quinn. *"Make certain he knows this must never happen again. The castle will never belong to him."*

Quinn nodded curtly and strode in front of the earl. When he got there, he yanked George's helmet off and tossed it into the dirt. George looked even worse than usual. His face was white, his eyes haunted. He'd seen things today he'd never forget.

"This ends here," Quinn thundered. "Do I make myself clear?"

"But James said—" George began.

Quinn backhanded him, leaving a raw spot across one cheekbone. "I don't give a jolly fuck what that poor excuse for a sovereign told you. We will spare your life today, and that of your remaining knights. If you chose to return, we shan't be as generous."

"I have nowhere else to go," he said quietly. It was probably the first honest thing out of him.

"You'll work it out," Quinn said.

"Because you have no choice," Rhiana cut in. "Now, begone."

"Wait!" I couldn't stand not having my voice, so I moved us to the form that's mostly me with him visible behind.

"Where'd the demons come from?" I asked.

He scrunched his face into a disgusted moue. "The king must have sent them. I swear I didn't know they'd be part of this until they showed up."

"It's a long way from Solway Moss to here," I pointed out. "Why did you not question how a company of soldiers arrived so quickly?"

His shoulders slumped still further. "I should have."

I had to know if he spoke true, so I scraped through his mind, not bothering to be gentle. He grabbed his head in both hands but didn't cry out.

"Any idea how James got so cozy with monsters?" was my next question.

George made the sign of the cross twice and shook his head.

"I'm done with you. Leave." I flapped a hand his way.

He narrowed his eyes. "You're monsters. How are you better than them?" He pointed at a fallen demon, black guts stinking where they scattered on the ground.

Quinn laughed as if George had told the richest of jokes. When he got hold of himself, he said, "Aye, mate, but we're the good monsters."

"You really should learn to tell the difference," Delilah simpered.

Roland flew past, narrowly missing George's ear with his snapping beak before landing on Quinn's shoulders.

"You will never return." I repeated Quinn's admonition.

George growled something I couldn't make out. Wheeling his black stallion, he led his knights away from the killing field.

Aidyrth swooped in for a landing. "Can you believe that?" she bugled.

"Believe what?" Quinn asked.

"The king of Scotland pulled men from a battle that's far from assured."

"It's the last bad decision he'll ever make," I grunted and let the wolf take over.

We made our way back to the castle after piling the demons onto a pyre lit by dragonfire. Aidyrth breathed a spell over it and instructed it to burn out once the last of the demons had been reduced to cinders. She withdrew the enchantment powering the other fires she'd lit.

We should torch the remaining bodies, about twenty of them, but it could wait. Coming across dead bodies was one thing. We didn't want mortals stumbling over hard evidence of demonkind.

Aidyrth ducked beneath the lintel. The castle's front doors were four meters high and made of richly carved wood, but they still weren't quite tall enough to accommodate her bulk.

"If any doubts remain about poisoning James—" Delilah muttered.

"No doubts." Still in wolf form, I resorted to telepathy.

Quinn showed up with two bottles under an arm. "A toast is in order," he said.

The wolf faded to where he lives within me. "Hang on," I told everyone. "Let me dress."

"What if we like the scenery better this way?" Delilah's lush mouth curved provocatively. Her smile triggered an immediate response. All the more reason to bolt upstairs and reclaim my garments. Guess I wasn't angry with her any longer.

Back on the ground floor, with my unruly appendage under wraps, I grabbed a glass and topped it up with sweet-smelling spirits.

"A toast to our new home," Quinn cried and lifted his goblet.

"And to the Circle of Assassins," Delilah added.

"I'll drink to that," I said and drained half my glass.

Aidyrth bugled. Dorcha whinnied. Roland cawed.

I set down my glass. "Hadn't planned on George showing up, but it's good he did."

"Aye, one less problem to worry about," Rhiana agreed.

"Do you think we got through to him?" I glanced around the group and saw nods.

"He's a man of God," Rhiana said slowly. "After what he saw today, he wouldn't want this castle back. He'll view it as tainted."

"Hope you're right," I said. "Meanwhile, James won't be around to add his evil minions to the mix." I shook my head. "How on earth did he forge an alliance with vampires and demons?"

"Weak men make shit decisions," Quinn mumbled. "I've seen it before."

"You'd questioned why all of us need to go to Falkland Palace in Fife," Delilah said. "After today, you can count on James being surrounded by his supernatural pets. They can sense magic."

"And poison," Rhiana added.

"Aye, you might have to pour it down his throat." Quinn slapped a thigh as if he'd just cracked the most amazing joke.

I'd been planning to accost him in Edinburgh. Delilah's reminder was timely.

The sun was long since down. "Do we still want to do this tonight?" I asked everyone.

"Better sooner than later," Quinn said.

"Word about today has already traveled," Dorcha whinnied.

"Demons are all connected with either Satan or his princes," Aidyrth bugled. "'Tis a sure bet their deaths have been noted."

"Someone will want revenge." Quinn's chiseled mouth split into an anticipatory smile.

I hadn't considered that angle, mostly because demons hadn't loomed large in my life—until now.

"Best get this show moving forward," I said.

"I would hunt first," the dragon bugled softly. "We leave in an hour."

Quinn and Rhiana huddled around the bottles of spirits. Dorcha and Roland followed the dragon out of the castle.

Delilah beckoned to me. Not knowing what she wanted, I followed her. My attraction hadn't dimmed much since the day we'd nearly made love, but I couldn't follow my dick around. Wanting her and it being wise weren't synonymous. Aye, 'twas my head talking. My body sang a different tune. Breath quickened as I watched the sway of her hips a few steps ahead.

"You were amazing on the field today," I said.

"Thank you. The River Ness likes me and is quite accommodating." Turning right, she led the way into the library. Still lined with generations of Gordon books and scrolls, it was crowded and smelled of ancient vellum.

"One day"—I spread my arms wide—"we'll have a magical library here, one we can refer to when needed."

She turned to me. "This is coming together splendidly. We feel like a family. I'd never have guessed our effort would gel so quickly."

"It is working out rather well," I agreed.

Delilah held out her hand and clasped one of mine. "I wanted to tell you again how sorry I am about what I did in the beginning. I have no idea what got into me except a misguided power grab. It won't happen again."

"No need to apologize—you already did. Besides, I trust you. If you didn't have faith in the Circle, you'd have argued against being part of it."

"Aidyrth is in with both wings, and all her teeth." Delilah laughed. "Even if I'd disagreed, it wouldn't have made much difference. Beyond my bond with her, I recognize value in us working together, and I'll do everything I can to make the Circle a success."

"If we have to fight our way out of a phalanx of vampires or demons, there's a river not too far from Fife Palace. Your water mage skills could be a great boon."

She angled her head to one side. "You appreciate me."

"Of course I do."

She squeezed my hand. "We got off to a rather unfortunate start, Grigori, but you're a very attractive man."

Deep inside, my wolf howled approval.

Delilah laughed, so she must have heard him.

Somehow, she ended up in my arms, all warmth and curves and the enticing scent of saltwater pounding on wet rocks. When she turned her face up, I crushed my mouth over hers and held her close.

Breasts crushed into my chest. She opened her mouth to my questing tongue. We stood there for a long while teasing one another with a kiss that developed a life of its own. Her nipples hardened against me, and my cock swelled, embarrassingly ready to do most anything.

My heart pounded against my ribs. My breathing had quickened when I cradled the back of her head in one hand and broke our kiss.

"Hang onto that thought," I told her.

"Does it mean we can pick up where we left off?" Her lips were swollen from kissing me, making her look even more desirable.

"I hope so."

The wolf howled once more with enthusiasm. My words had been quite the understatement. I'd longed for Delilah in my arms since our first tryst. One more reason to put the James problem to bed once and for all. The Circle could get on to more important matters, and she and I would be endlessly inventive.

Reaching down, I swatted her high, tight bottom and let go of her while I still could. Willpower only goes so far.

"Time to meet the others and leave. Let's get this next task behind us."

She grinned. "I do believe you're looking forward to forcing James's mouth open and pouring Rhiana's concoction down his gullet."

I snorted. "You have no idea."

Usually, killing's not personal for me. This instance was totally different. I wanted James deader than dead. Plus, I wanted him to suffer. Unfortunately, Rhiana's poison wouldn't offer much opportunity for misery, but I'd take what I could get. Quick might be a good thing if a group of demons showed up, any of whom might possess an antidote.

"Oh, I think I do." Silvery laughter warmed me.

Hand in hand, we went in search of the rest of the Circle.

few hours of darkness remained when we emerged
into the thick wood between Falkland Palace and
the River Eden. Delilah slipped away toward the
river to harness its spirit to her bidding.

Everyone's magic was damped down to bare minimums.
We finalized our plans. Nothing elaborate. The others would
wait for my signal. If my efforts went smoothly, I'd rejoin
them, and we'd teleport the hell out of here. Just in case I ran
into problems, Delilah was courting the river. Rhiana
encouraged her affinity with fire and air. Quinn reached deep
into the earth.

We were covered with all four elements should we require
their power. None of them suffer demons willingly. Or
vampires, either. Another argument for the Circle. Other
than Rhiana—and there are damned few elemental mages
around—none of us commanded all the elements. I'm at the
bottom of the magical totem pole in that regard since I don't

control a one. I can call on earth power. If it's in a generous mood, it will accommodate me.

My lack of an assured connection with the elements has never stopped me, but I've never killed a king before, either. Things come full circle. I'd transitioned from killing for kings to knocking one off. It didn't bother me in the least. Not after all the crap James had chucked my way. If I'd been inclined toward clemency, his last stunt where he used George Gordon to get to me had sealed his future, or lack of one to put a finer point on it.

After shrouding myself in invisibility, I mounted the hill leading to the palace. It was constructed in such a way to confer protection should it be attacked. I snuck past the palace guard. They were dozing, and I was both silent and hidden from view.

I considered checking for other iterations of supernaturals but didn't. I was as prepared as I could be. If I ran into opposition, I'd deal with it as it arose. Some things aren't amenable to planning. If the others had come inside with me, it would have put a different slant on things. We'd have assigned roles, and seeking out vamps and demons would have been front and center.

I've never been inside this palace before, but most of them are laid out similarly. With the exception of Inverness Castle, royalty tends to maintain bedchambers on the lower levels to facilitate escape via a warren of underground tunnels. Most castles had them.

Creeping through the bottom floor, I passed the great room, a couple of drawing rooms, a study, and steps that led to the kitchens judging from the smells of food. While not as grand as Edinburgh Castle, the palace was thoughtfully appointed with marble floors, suits of armor at intervals, and wall hangings. The remains of the previous evening's fires smoldered in hearths in every room.

An unusual scent nagged me until I identified it as opium. I stifled a sigh before it escaped. Had James added drugs to his list of unkingly traits? His queen had just given birth. Any father worth his salt would have been present for the birth, or, failing that, would have hustled home.

The babe was his first legitimate heir. Perhaps all the illegitimate ones had hardened him to the miracle that his queen had finally managed to birth a babe after many miscarriages.

I yanked my mind back to why I was here. So far, the ground floor hadn't yielded anything. I'd already been inside longer than I'd planned, so I released a faint tracking spell to locate my prey. As soon as it vibrated, I released it.

Any magic at all would draw attention my way—if anyone were looking.

I'd been on the right track about his bedchamber being on this floor. I just hadn't gone far enough. Backtracking to a side corridor I'd ignored earlier, I deepened my warding and glided across flooring that had turned to wood covered by rugs.

The opium smell was stronger here. And I smelled James. Never especially careful with grooming, he made up the difference with cologne. The result was reminiscent of a cheap whore coating the musk of her trade with flowery scents. The corridor was deserted.

So far, so good.

Within me, the wolf's senses were deployed. I sensed his edginess. Something about this bothered him, but he kept his concerns to himself. A single door at the end of the hallway was closed. James was on the other side.

I flattened myself against a wall and took a moment to listen. The soft murmur of voices suggested James's usual harem was in attendance. I'd have to scrub a bunch of minds before this was over.

Not impossible, but not part of my game plan, either.

Aye, about my lack of a plan. Was I going to burst through the door and manhandle James until the poison was administered? The idea of witnesses didn't appeal to me.

I had to release my warding at some point.

An idea rattled about. It would have to do. Nothing like pretending business as usual. Striding forward, I knocked before pushing the door open. The combined stench of opium and sex gagged me. I breathed shallowly through my mouth to mitigate the worst of it.

James lolled on an enormous bed with silken hangings. Four women, all naked, fawned over him. One rode him. Another knelt between his legs taking turns licking both him and the woman above him. The other two swayed to a tune only they could hear as they pleasured themselves for him to watch.

Despite my knock, no one noticed me. Of course not. They couldn't see me. Apparently, no one had heard my fist on the door, either. They were too intoxicated to be aware of anything. Poppies are far worse than spirits in that regard.

I released my warding, pushed the door shut, and approached the bed.

"James." My tone was gruff.

His head twisted slowly on its scrawny stalk of a neck. He

pried his eyes open and groaned. "For the love of God, why aren't you dead yet?"

"Because you keep hiring inferiors to do the job," I said cheerfully.

Time for a private tete-a-tete. I snapped my fingers. "Ladies. Leave us." Because I seeded my words with compulsion, they wandered out of the room. The one who'd been on top of James left last. All were sunk in a hazy dreamlike state courtesy of the opium.

Perhaps clearing their memories of me would be simpler than I expected.

"Go away." He flapped a hand in my direction.

His flippant attitude annoyed me. Reaching to grab his shoulders, I pulled him into a sit and tossed him back against the wall. Thumping his naked chest with my index finger, I snarled, "Why did you send your troops against me?"

He snaked a hand toward a golden bell on a bedside table. I snatched my dirk from a thigh sheath and skewered his hand with it. My next move was to drape a hasty sound shield over us.

"Holler all you want," I suggested silkily. "No one will hear you."

The beginnings of fear shadowed his befuddled gaze. He shrank away from me.

"I asked a question." Another chest thump.

"George came to me for help. I am his king, so I provided troops."

"Did you happen to mention you'd promised Inverness Castle to me?"

He looked away. "Um, can't we just forget this? It's been a bad day. The queen birthed a girl." His face twisted into a rictus of disgust. "A girl. After all the dead ones, this is what I get? And we're losing on Solway Moss."

"If you'd left troops there and not diverted them to harass me, Solway might have a better outcome."

A flood of words wanted out. I ached to tell him what a poor excuse for a monarch he was, but none of it mattered.

Lunging forward, I pinned him against the wall with one hand. He writhed beneath my grip and cried for his guards. They couldn't hear him. I'd told him as much, but he'd never been a good listener.

In one quick motion, I retrieved the vial of Rhiana's potion, pulled the stopper with my teeth, forced his mouth open, and poured it inside. He fought me then, but the contest was absurd. I chucked the vial aside to free my other hand to keep his mouth shut. Whether he swallowed or not wouldn't alter the outcome. The poison would soak in through his gums.

A quick trip through his mind yielded confusion. Why was I doing this?

How could he not know?

His struggles were weakening. Another minute or two, and I could release him, retrace my steps, and be gone. He sagged in my grasp. I let go and left the chamber. The women were huddled around the door.

I hadn't forgotten about them, but neither could I leave their fuzzed out minds alone. Murdering them was overkill, so I scrubbed their minds. They'd forget far more than tonight, but at least they'd remember who they were.

Generous of me.

Pleased with what had turned out to be a solid night's work, I reconstructed my ward and exited the castle. The guard were still asleep. No one would even know I'd been here. I waited until I was at the bottom of the hill to release my concealment spell.

Satisfied I'd done Scotland a good turn, I joined the others. They milled about exactly where I'd left them, wearing grim expressions.

"What's wrong?" I asked. "James is dead. Everything went well."

"Until you left," Rhiana muttered darkly.

"Aye, Vampires showed up on the heels of your departure. They're turning James into one of them." Quinn spat into the dirt.

"But he was dead when I left him," I protested.

"Not dead enough," Dorcha whinnied.

"We have to go back," I said.

"Aye, we were waiting on you," Delilah informed me.

"Vampires must have been here all along," Aidyrth bugled softly. "They can sense death. It's how they locate easy prey and swell their ranks."

A spell built around me. I trusted whoever was crafting it. "Back to the bedchamber?" I asked.

"Where else?" Delilah grinned.

A quick blast of magic encompassed everyone except the dragon. "I'll take care of things from the outside," she reassured us.

The forest liquified. When the world came into focus, I was back in James's bedchamber. Two male vampires garbed in priest's robes hovered over him, holding wrists streaming with black blood to his mouth. Damn but they're beautiful creatures. Perfectly formed. Flawless, actually. The irony of them masquerading as holy men wasn't lost on me.

One had coal black hair and penetrating dark eyes. The other's hair was russet. His head was turned away from me, so I couldn't make out anything else.

James seemed to be having trouble swallowing. Perhaps Rhiana's poison got in the way. Or maybe, just maybe, he was struggling with signing on with evil. Being pathetic and inadequate was one thing. Transforming into an abomination quite another.

The vampires barely glanced our way. Both of them hissed. "He is ours, now," in oddly discordant tones.

"We'll see about that," Rhiana declared.

She and Quinn joined hands. The floor rolled beneath our feet as floorboards cracked from the pressure of their combined magic. Distant screams from elsewhere in the palace suggested guests were fleeing on the heels of what they assumed was an earthquake.

Windows in the far wall shattered. Aidyrth stuck her head through and scoured the vampires with fire. They didn't burn. Interesting. I hadn't known they were impervious to flames. Other items in the chamber didn't fare nearly as well. Tables and chairs caught fire. The curtains turned into charred strips of fabric. Delilah coaxed water from somewhere to quench the worst of the inferno before the space became uninhabitable.

The vampires were crooning over James in a language I've never heard. Simple enough to guess what they said. They had to be exhorting him to try harder. Something clicked, and his body jerked upright. Mouth smeared with blood, he could have been the boogie man in every child's worst nightmare.

He bounded off the bed, swaying on his feet. The vampires sat back, pleased expressions on their undead faces as they sealed their flowing wrists. "You're one of us now," the dark-haired one intoned.

"Who do you want to feed from first?" the other simpered.

James fastened his hollow-eyed gaze on me. I recognize bloodlust when I see it. Newly formed vampires have no restraint. Usually, they're forced to remain within the seethe until they develop control over their feeding habits.

I readied myself to meet his attack head on. I'd killed him once; I could do it again.

He rushed me, mouth open, jaws clacking in a frantic search for something to glom onto. His vacant eyes glittered with madness. Probably his feeble brain wasn't capable of the transformation. Many brand-new vamps don't make it. They sink into insanity, and their kinsmen make short work of them.

Ha. I'd save them the trouble. James's arms flailed against my chest. He hooked a foot around one of my ankles, jaws still flapping frantically.

"Opening your doors to evil is the last mistake you'll ever make." I aimed my words right at him; they rolled off. I doubt he heard a one.

Tired of this man-child's antics, I did what I should have done the first time. Gripping his head in both hands, I twisted it until the satisfying crunch of vertebrae breaking told me his spinal cord was no more. I kept right on twisting and tugging until his head came off in my hands.

Blood slewed everywhere. Hot and reeking of dead things. It wasn't yet black. That part of the change took time. I kept hold of his head. His body crumpled to the floor.

The other vampires looked on. Clearly, James wasn't much of a loss to them.

Dorcha held back, surveying the scene.

Fists pounded on the wooden doors of James's chamber.

"Sire. Sire. Are you all right?"

"We've come to lead you to safety."

I could marvel later that anyone who worked for him wouldn't rejoice in his demise. For now, I sent a bolt of magic to boobytrap the door. The next time someone touched it, I heard a screech, followed by a yelp. Heavy footsteps pounded away.

Rhiana beckoned to her bondmate. "Finish this."

With an eager whinny, Dorcha bounded forward. I've seen unicorns kill before. They're truly a thing of beauty. With no wasted motion, Dorcha covered all three vampires with silvery netting. In James's case, the netting wrapped around his body. I still had hold of his head. Once the two live ones writhed like gutted fish, she sank her horn into their hearts one after the other.

"Drop the head," she whinnied.

I tossed it atop the ruin of what had been James's body. She impaled him, and then stepped back. Her horn glistened with black blood. She did a little two-step with her hoofs to avoid tracking through the worst of it.

If the chamber smelled bad before, the stench had expanded to atrocious. Residual opium, unwashed bodies, tacky sex. A fitting end for James.

"All done here," Dorcha neighed.

Her netting vanished. The two older vampires crumpled to the ground. James's body looked the same. The others degraded to piles of bones before my eyes. They must have been old.

Aidyrth's head was still stuck through the window. The unmistakable feel of dragon magic wafted through the room. I stepped over broken floorboards to form a tight knot with the others.

The best part of that stinking space retreating was the smell went along with it. Not that we didn't reek, but the worst of the stench stayed in the chamber. When Aidyrth released us, it was on the banks of the River Ness. All of us shed our clothes and washed in its waters.

"How'd you know about the vampires?" I asked Rhiana.

"We watched you the whole time," she said.

"Aye, good thing we kept on watching after you left," Quinn muttered.

"Fortuitous, indeed," Delilah said.

I walked out of the river, shaking droplets from my body and hair. The night was cold, but it felt cleansing after the fetid closeness of Falkland Palace.

The wolf wanted out. Hunting was high on his priority list.

Delilah hip-butted me. "What's next?"

Her meaning was abundantly clear. I hip-butted back. "Patience, darling."

"Och, that's no fun," she teased.

I motioned everyone into a circle. "We need food and rest. Let's regroup this evening in the castle."

"We can plan our next project," Quinn said.

"We'll make a list," Rhiana said firmly. "And prioritize from there."

Quinn bowed her way. "I defer to you, Madam Elemental Mage."

She rolled her eyes. "We worked well together back there. I respect the way you hold power."

"It's mutual."

"Working together will become second nature, the more we do it," I told the group.

"I'm going hunting," the dragon announced, spread her wings, and vanished. Wherever she planned to hunt, it wasn't here.

"Me too." Dorcha shook water from her mane and took off at a gallop.

Quinn and Rhiana picked up their clothes and headed for the castle.

"On a more serious note, what do you want to do?" Delilah asked softly and gathered her clothes.

"My wolf wants out. Will you hunt with us?"

Her eyes rounded in surprise. "Not the answer I expected, but sure. I've never hunted with a werewolf."

"Makes two of us. I've always hunted alone in wolf form."

The wolf was done with idle prattle. After forcing his way through, he swiped his tongue over Delilah's face and took off at a sedate pace. She tugged clothing on over her wet body and followed in his wake.

"Do you want me to collect your garments?" she asked.

"Nay, I'll get them later. Thank you for asking, though."

Rather than settling into a wolfy lope that ate up miles, the wolf walked slowly. He'd wait for Delilah. Even offer her choice bits from his kills. When they were done communing, we'd see what materialized.

The wolf sometimes complained he never got to know the

odd woman in my life. My response had always been it wasn't worth his time since none of them moved beyond one-night-stand status.

He'd decided to do things differently this time; he's wise and must have had reasons. It got me thinking as he pounced and killed, ate and repeated the cycle. By the time we meandered back to the riverbank where my filthy clothing was, I had the beginnings of a strategy in place.

19

Back in mortal form, I picked up my garments and tucked them under one arm. They were so dirty, I couldn't bear the thought of putting them back on. Dawn wasn't far off. The edges of the eastern sky were developing pearlescent edges.

"How'd you like the hunt?" I asked Delilah as we started for the castle gates. Someone had closed them. Wise of them.

She was still sucking tender bits from her fingers. "Lovely. I'd never have guessed how succulent raw rabbit meat is."

"The wolf took good care of you," I told her.

She cocked her head to one side and looked at me. "Did I get special treatment?"

"Very."

"Why?"

"He likes you. So do I." I uttered a few words, and the gates swung inward. We walked through. A slight zing told me the protective spell around the castle was in place and active.

"There's a but hiding behind those words." She smiled softly and used magic of her own to seal the gates.

"Let's go inside. We can cozy up in front of a fire and talk."

Her brow crinkled in what might have been confusion. "All right. Talk it is. Do you want mead or other spirits?"

Bending, I kissed the top of her head. "Surprise me. Let's meet in the study on the second floor. The one overlooking the gardens. I'm going in search of clean clothes."

I expected a crack about not bothering to cover up. It never came. I mounted the stairs heading for the possessions I'd transferred from the humble shepherd's hut.

Was I making a mistake?

I'd never bothered talking with a woman beforehand about anything significant. We'd tumbled into bed, and that had been the beginning and end of it. Still, the wolf hadn't wooed any of them.

Delilah could become an important part of my life. I had to know if she felt the same, or if I was just one more man to her. In much the same way as I'd always viewed women. A means to an end. Not that I was ever unkind. Or uncaring. More indifferent.

I tossed on a pair of tan woolen breeks and a soft off-white woolen shirt. After stuffing my feet into battered sheepskin slippers, I walked down the hall to the study.

Delilah knelt on a cushion in front of the hearth. She'd already lit a fire; it crackled invitingly. An amber bottle of mead sat on a low table with two full glasses next to it.

"Come sit." She patted a pillow next to hers.

"Thank you. This is lovely." I folded my legs into a crouch and settled onto the colorful cushion.

Delilah grabbed one of the goblets and handed it to me. "Been a busy day. This was our first major undertaking."

"We worked well together. It's encouraging. Means we can add to our ranks."

She nodded. "That's right. You worked out some sort of deal with potential bond animals."

"Aye, I did." Angling my head to one side, I said, "You don't have to tell me, but how did you end up bonded with Aidyrth?"

A small shrug. "Who knows how these things happen? We were thrown together during the last dwarf war, and we clicked. It took about fifty years before we formalized our bond, though." She stopped for a moment and closed her teeth over her lower lip. "It makes me wonder how well instant pairings are going to work."

"Some of them probably won't," I agreed. "Still, mages who maintain a bond are a cut above. They're who I want in the Circle."

"I'm surprised you didn't ask how dragons got involved in the war between dwarfs and Fae."

"Now that you mention it"—I smiled, pleased by the easy camaraderie between us—"dragons aren't known for lifting a claw for non-dragons."

A corner of her mouth twitched. "Simple enough. The dwarfs promised them silver for their hoards. When they welched, the dragons merrily switched sides and buried thousands of dwarfs in their caves."

"When exactly did you and Aidyrth meet?"

"Right about the time the dragons discovered there was no silver to be had. She was so incensed, I expected all that fire inside would burn her to a cinder. Obviously, it didn't.

When she calmed down a little, she needed someone to talk with. I was there."

I sipped from my goblet, savoring the flowery honey drink.

"The dragon is immortal," Delilah went on. "While I am long lived, there will be a time when she must press forward without me. It was her only reservation before formalizing our bond."

After setting down my drink, I reached for her hand. She clasped mine.

"This is new for me," I murmured. "I have no idea what the future holds—for either of us—but I want you to be a part of my life."

"You don't know me very well," she observed. "We got off to a rocky start because of my greed."

"All true." I smoothed hair back from her face with my other hand. "We may decide being other than comrades in arms is a mistake, but I want more than a single night with you."

She laughed, the sound reminiscent of a wind chime. "Isn't this usually the conversation one has after sex?"

Her joy was infectious, and I grinned. "Aye, but I've always gotten to the bed part and never beyond. This time, I'm doing things differently."

"I'm glad. I want to be special to you."

I opened my arms. She drained half her glass, set it down, and snuggled close. For a time, we sat like that watching the fire. Having her by my side felt right in a way I'd never experienced. The wolf woofed softly, his happy woof and one I rarely heard.

I wanted her, but this was different. The frantic pressure

to jump into bed and get the whole thing over with wasn't there. The press of her body next to me, the scents of the sea, her silken hair floating this way and that. I noticed each detail, savoring it before moving to the next.

"You haven't told me about you," she murmured and curled a hand around my thigh.

I must have stiffened because she asked, "Did I say something wrong?"

"Not at all. No one's ever asked before, so it surprised me."

"No one's ever wanted to know about you?"

I chuckled. "It sounds so stark when you say it like that. Back when werewolves remained in a pack, we all knew everything there was to know about each other. We might have continued as we were, had Anubis not shown up. Hindsight is always crystal clear, but we should have refused to work for him."

I shook my head. "We all breathed a collective sigh when he left Earth. I'm still finding it tough to believe he returned and treated his minions so badly."

"That problem isn't exactly over," she murmured, "but go on."

It wasn't. Werewolves remained imprisoned somewhere. They were on my list whether or not that task rose to significance on the master list we constructed this evening.

"Agreed," I said. "I'm not used to talking about myself. My early years were spent with my kinsmen. After Anubis left, we remained in a pack for a while, but eventually disbanded and went separate ways."

"Why? Seems there's safety in numbers."

"Not for werewolves," I replied. "Mortals feared us.

Simpler to spend more and more time in our human bodies. Our wolves were miserable. The only way to allow them more roaming time was to split up. A lone wolf doesn't garner much attention. A pack of fifty or more is cause for alarm."

"Where'd you go after your pack split up?"

I cupped one side of her face and gazed at her. "Are you really interested?"

"Of course. I want to know everything about you."

Her words resonated in my core. The wolf howled happily.

"Many places. We traveled to several borderworlds, bouncing between them and Earth. Around the 1300s, I stumbled on the assassin trade. It was raw then, in its infancy. Simple to ingratiate myself with kings spread throughout Europe and the Ottoman Empire. Eventually, I moved to the British Isles."

"Have you been alone all this time?" she asked softly.

"I'm never alone," I corrected her. "The wolf is always with me."

She laced her fingers with mine. "Not what I meant, and you know as much."

"I've never remained in one place long enough. Once, long ago, there was a mortal woman who, well who died. It reminded me not to get attached."

"I'll die someday."

"Aye, but not for a long while. Besides, you command magic." I hesitated for a moment before continuing. "It's important."

Delilah nodded. "I understand. Once, when I was very young, a mortal man, an earl, fell in love with me. Flattered, I encouraged him foolishly believing he'd accept all of me." She made a sour face. "The moment he caught me practicing magic, he turned me in to the local priest, who tried to burn me at the stake."

"I'd like to have seen that."

"Aye, it wasn't pretty. I murdered the priest and his twisted acolytes, and then I called a nearby river. It flooded the fields. That town went hungry after winter came. They're fortunate I didn't do more."

She tilted her chin at a defiant angle. "It was the beginning of my stint as an assassin. All of that happened long before I joined forces with Aidyrth, though."

"I like that story. In truth, I want to know how everyone in the Circle was called to our trade."

"I'm certain they'll oblige." She reached into the emerald-green robe she'd changed into and pulled out a small flask. I only just now noticed she wasn't dressed in the same clothing she'd worn to Falkland Palace.

"Mead wasn't the only thing I brought. Take off your shirt. Let me rub this oil into your skin." She unstoppered the vial. Scents of vanilla, mint, and bayberry tickled my nostrils.

I let go of her and pulled the woolen garment over my head. After giving the fire a shot of magic to encourage a hardier blaze, I lay on my stomach with my head on the pillow I'd been sitting on.

She straddled my ass. Warm oil drizzled down my spine. Delilah chanted a tuneless melody that soothed my mind and spirit. It ebbed and flowed with the power of many oceans. Strong fingers worked oil into the muscles of my shoulders, arms, and back.

No one has ever pampered me. After a brief period where I felt uncomfortable, perhaps unworthy, I soaked up the attention, loving the feel of her touch as she found tense places I didn't know I had and coaxed the strain from them.

After a time, she lay full length on top of me. It was then I realized she'd opened her robe. Bare breasts pressed into my shoulders as she rubbed her flesh over mine. Twisting, I wrapped my arms around her and held her tight. Her mouth sought mine. I tangled my fingers in her long, lush hair.

Her skin was tantalizing, enticing. I pressed my tongue against the seam of her lips. She opened her mouth and teased my tongue with hers. Between us, my cock swelled to fullness. She wrapped her legs around one of my thighs, and the heat of her core seared my skin.

Sounds came from me, wolfy noises I'd never uttered in this body. In between kisses, I howled softly. Delilah plumbed a place deep within me, a spot no one had touched before. In that moment, I understood how well I'd always protected myself, and how those protections had assured no one would ever get close enough to harm me.

Living and loving come with risks. For the first time, I embraced all of them as I embraced the mage in my arms. Her breasts and belly were slick with oil from my back. Our bodies slid against each other, the scent from the oil growing with our mounting desire.

She swiped her tongue around my mouth, bit my lower lip, and broke our kiss to sit over me. Her robe slipped from her shoulders revealing high full breasts with coppery nipples. She had broad shoulders for a woman, and a sculpted ribcage. Her arms were shapely with muscle, her stomach flat, her hips flared.

Her fingers were busy undoing my breeks, which she slid down my legs.

Drinking her in by the light of the flickering fire was ambrosial.

"My life has never been so rich," I murmured, my voice raspy with unmet need.

She ran her fingertips up my distended shaft. "Mine, either." This time, she cradled my newly uncovered erection with an oil-saturated hand. The slick sensation of flesh on flesh took my breath away.

I filled my hands with her breasts, tweaking and pinching her nipples. They grew long and hard beneath my ministrations. She groaned and buried her other hand between her legs. Rosy patches splotched her breasts and face.

Letting go of her breasts, I tugged at the hand working herself. Once I'd extricated it, I pulled it to my mouth and licked nectar off her fingers. The deep, musky scent and taste of her got to me.

No more waiting. I circled her waist with both hands and lifted her onto my cock pushing all the way into the wonder of her body. She gasped and balanced herself with her hands on my shoulders. Her hair fell all around us creating a curtain of golden silk.

She rose until only the tip of me was inside, and then slowly took me in again. I let her set the pace, but her agonizingly slow movements disintegrated after half a dozen strokes. Panting, moaning, and rocking against me, she moved faster and faster until her body dissolved in a pool of molten heat.

I held back. Gods, it wasn't easy. I couldn't recall when I'd last made love. When she began moving again, I met her stroke for stroke. Our bodies strained together as lust built, taking me higher than I'd ever been.

"Come with me." Her voice was so ragged it was barely there. "Now."

Maybe she used magic. None of it mattered. When I felt her contract around me, I released my control. Jism juddered from me. I came for a long time, savoring each twitch, each spasm. They brought me closer to the woman in my arms.

I wound my arms around her. She lay on top of me with my cock still buried in her body. After our breathing quieted, we might have dozed.

"Thank you." The wolf's voice woke me.

"For what?"

"Not running away this time."

"I second that." Delilah's voice was husky with spent passion. "Thank you for taking a chance on me."

"Flows both ways." I covered her mouth with mine. When I was done kissing her, I asked, "Ready to find a bed?"

She nodded. "We can pick pretty much anything."

"Your choice. The important thing for me is that you're there."

She wriggled out of my embrace and rolled away from me to a sit. "Aw, bet you say that to all the girls."

"You'd lose that bet."

I got my feet under me and stood. Extending a hand, I helped her up and wove an arm around her waist. We wandered out of the study. I'd meant what I said. Rooms aren't important to me, neither are beds.

"If they're not, what is?" she asked.

"Kiping thoughts, eh?"

"It's instructive. Answer the question."

I turned and wrapped my arms around her. "You're important."

"So are you, to me. Now let go so I can find us a landing spot."

I walked by her side until she said, "This one," and followed her into a lushly appointed bedchamber. One that might have belonged to George's wife.

"Perfect choice." I joined her on a bed of ermine and white fox. The day was young. With luck, we'd have a few more opportunities before it was time to meet everyone over dinner.

"I like the way you think," she murmured and tossed a leg over me.

"Guess I'm stuck with you in my head," I teased.

"Any complaints?" she arched a fair brow.

"None at all." I laughed and drew her nearer still.

20

We joined the others in one of the dining rooms and found an impressive spread of food. Liliane and Jonas had been busy. Apparently, Liliane had done most of the cooking for her father's tavern. Chicken and dumplings simmered in a pot on the hearth. Fresh bread and cheese sat on a wooden trencher along with olives and nuts.

We'd have to find sources of foodstuffs to keep us since the neighboring serfs had probably fled along with their master, the Earl of Huntly. I added it to a mental list.

News about supernaturals spreads like wildfire, and most mortals wouldn't willingly remain in proximity to us. Not this generation. By the time subsequent ones came along with no untoward events attributable to Inverness Castle, we'd smooth the waters.

"We were wondering if you were going to show up." Rhiana cast a pointed glance our way.

"Aye, the entire castle reeks of sex," Quinn joked.

"Isn't anyone going to wish us well?" I inquired.

"Told you." Dorcha prodded her bondmate with her horn. "It is serious."

Aidyrth stalked forward from a corner where she'd been hunched. The ceiling needed to be half a meter taller to comfortably accommodate her. "Approach me," she commanded, her words aimed dead at me.

I did and stood quietly beneath her scrutiny. Dragon magic scoured me. It wasn't comfortable, but I endured her examination. "Your attentions are honorable," she announced. Relief rode beneath her words.

I nodded. "Aye. No harm shall befall Delilah if I can help it. My wolf feels the same."

Delilah joined me and bowed to her bondmate. "Thank you," she said.

"Why didn't you talk with me first?" the dragon demanded.

Delilah trained her blue eyes on Aidyrth. "Because I did not know."

"And you do now?" A scaled brow creaked upward.

Delilah turned to me and smiled. "We're finding our way," she said. Turning to face the others, she added, "This makes no difference in my role. Grigori leads the Circle. I will not receive special treatment."

"I don't know about leading," I spoke up. "I view the Circle as a joint effort including us all. We have equal voices, but in case of a disagreement we cannot overcome, I may step in."

"Good to know," Quinn said gruffly.

I filled a bowl with the chicken dish and a plate with

bread, butter, and cheese. Delilah did the same. We joined the others at a rectangular wooden table.

The dragon lumbered closer. "Before you arrived," she announced, "we'd begun a task list."

I nodded and continued eating.

"Top of the list," Rhiana said, "is recruiting more of us."

Dorcha pawed at the floor, making a scritching sound. "The zebra who greeted you in the animals' world contacted me asking why she hasn't heard from you."

I chewed and swallowed. "What'd you tell her?"

"That we're still developing the concept, but we'll be adding to our ranks soon."

Pleased the zebra had reached out, I hurried to finish my meal. During my two visits to the animals' realm, I hadn't been certain she welcomed the idea of providing bondmates for future Circle members.

"While you were, um, otherwise occupied, I reached out to a few mates." Quinn showed unusual restraint. He wasn't unduly crass, neither did he chide me for taking a few hours for myself. Had the shoe been on the other foot, he'd still be in bed, but I didn't mention it.

"And?" I sopped up the last of my soup with a chunk of bread.

"Found another earth mage and a couple of shifters who might be interested. The mage is in China, the shifters are in Egypt. They wouldn't require animals, but the mage would. They'll be here as soon as they can to firm up details."

I stood and walked to the front of the table where I could see everyone. Roland chose that moment to fly through an open window with a dead something-or-other clutched in his hooked beak. He dropped it in front of the dragon and fluttered to the table where he lit next to the soup pot. Dipping his beak, he came up with a bit of chicken.

"Did I miss anything?" he croaked.

Quinn stroked a wing. "Nay. Right on time."

We were all here. Excellent. I selected my next words with care.

"So far, we're decently matched and work well together. I'm all for adding to the Circle but with the following caveat. We will vote on each recruit. If even one of us has reservations, we will not add them to the Circle."

"What about a simple majority?" Quinn asked.

I nodded. "The problem with that is if one of us vetoes someone, there will be friction between them. Do you want to be part of a group where you're not 100 percent in favor of the mage who might work alongside you?"

"I agree," Rhiana said. "No rush getting bigger. I asked around too, and three elemental mages were interested. Unfortunately, two of them are impossible to work with unless they're on top of the heap."

"What did you tell them?" I asked.

"That I'd be in touch." She smiled.

"Not that this is any of my affair," I said, "but where did you even find other elemental mages? I thought you were the only one left on Earth."

She cast a pointed glance my way. "I am."

I got the picture and didn't press for further information.

"Next order of business," I said, "is do we prioritize adding mages to the Circle or taking on tasks?"

"Why can't we do both?" Delilah asked. She'd finished eating and was working on a goblet of mead.

"We can," I replied. "If everyone agrees."

Between nods and ayes, consensus pointed to doing it all.

"The last thing I want to bring up," I said, "is whether we want to court business from monarchs. When I thought up the idea for the Circle, I assumed we'd mainly do what I've been doing for centuries: acting as court assassins. But that was before I slaughtered James."

"It's where my money comes from," Rhiana said. "When Dorcha and I aren't hanging out at carnivals."

The unicorn neighed loudly. "I hate that. I have to adopt a glamour so people see me as a horse. It's demeaning running around in circles under a canvas tent."

Rhiana rose and draped an arm around Dorcha's neck. "I know, I know." Her tone was soothing. "But it's maintained a roof over our heads when times were lean."

Dorcha stamped a hoof.

I kept my thoughts to myself. Money wasn't usually a problem for mages. Why'd Rhiana feel the need to moonlight as a carnival act? Granted, I did live better by dint of my court-related assignments, but I wouldn't stave without them.

Rhiana let go of her bondmate. "No one will know who killed James. They'll find evidence of an earthquake and vampiric activity. If we want to curry favor in Europe's courts, that door is still wide open."

"I didn't think it would be closed," I told her. "My concern is whether I want to hire out to royalty again."

"Eh, they're all a bunch of stuffed geese," Quinn muttered. "I say we take work where we can get it. Most of our internal projects won't produce income." Spreading his arms wide, he went on, "This castle will be expensive to maintain. Before, you had a room in James's castle with no overhead."

"Good point. Thanks for the reality check." I stopped there. We'd covered enough ground.

"So where are we?" Quinn asked.

"We're here," I replied. "Recapping our discussion, new recruits are accepted by unanimous vote."

"It should be the same for new bond animals." Roland clacked his beak.

"Aye, you're not the only ones who don't always get along," Dorcha whinnied.

"Glad you brought it up," Aidyrth bugled.

I thought about their request. "In terms of order," I said slowly, "if a mage is interested, and they're not already associated with an animal, their first stop is the animals' world. Once bonded, they'll spend time here—not sure how much—and then we'll vote."

"How should we package it?" Rhiana asked.

"Honestly," I replied. "We tell everyone the truth. Worst case scenario, a mage garners a new bondmate. It will enrich their lives even if they're not a fit for the Circle."

"What if the match falls apart?" Delilah asked. "Most of us spent years deciding to formalize our bonds. We're asking both the animal and the mage for a much shorter timeline."

"We'll tackle that problem when we have to." Crossing to the food table, I poured myself a glass of mead and swallowed half of it. "We'll never hammer out every fine point. Not today, or next week. Some problems will have to present themselves before we come up with solutions."

Delilah grinned crookedly. "I like things tacked down. Feel free to call me on it if it gets in the way. Who's going to develop new court affiliations?"

"Hopefully, all of us," I replied. "It can be one of our next tasks before we tackle the Dark Fae or missing werewolves or some other mage problem. Tomorrow each of us will pay a visit to whichever courts you've done assassin work for. Inform your contacts you're available, and that you've teamed up with several others like you, so future jobs will be quick and clean."

"What will you do about James?" Quinn arched both dark brows.

"Play dumb. I'll show up at Edinburgh looking for him. When they tell me he's dead—"

"They might not know so soon," Quinn cut in.

I nodded. "Regardless, I'll congratulate them on the birth of James's heir and remind them I'm available to deal with any difficulties." I paused to take a breath, and then added. "Pretty certain they'll hire us to deal with their vampire problem. If not tomorrow, then whenever they put two and two together and ascertain vamps were responsible for James's untimely demise."

I grabbed the mead bottle and plunked it on the table. "I'd like to propose a toast. Fill your glasses."

When the bottle ran dry, I got another from the cellars. Once everyone was ready, I raised my glass. "I propose a toast to the Circle of Assassins. May we prosper and enrich each other's lives."

Cries of, "To the Circle," rang around the room.

I sat next to Delilah. We'd accomplished a great deal today and agreed on almost everything. The Circle had a home in Inverness Castle. We had goals. It was a start.

Being immortal confers time. Clarifying every single detail today wasn't necessary. Mages and animals were chatting and finishing off the food. Before we retired for the evening, I had one last thing to say.

Back on my feet, I tapped on a goblet to snag everyone's attention. "Don't get the idea I'm hogging the limelight," I joked. "I never did thank all of you for taking a chance on my untried and unproven concept. I hope the Circle flourishes. If it does, it will be because each of you added grit and heart to it.

"This won't be easy. We'll run into mages stronger than us, and monarchs who deserve James's fate. Through it all, we'll persevere so long as we're open and honest. If something doesn't resonate with you, step up and tell me. Better yet, tell the group.

"The more decisions we make together, the stronger we'll be."

I sat back down. Sometimes more words muddy the waters, and I'd said enough. Delilah placed a hand over mine and leaned into me.

"After our court visits tomorrow," Rhiana said, "can we take a look at the group of Dark Fae blocking access to the eastern borderworlds?"

I got back to my feet. "Erm, I know I said I was done, but one of the reasons I originally settled on Inverness Castle is it sits atop a gateway that will make accessing borderworlds much simpler."

Rhiana looked surprised. Clearly she hadn't known. Aidyrth did, but not her. "Thanks, Grigori. How about my proposal to deal with the Dark Fae?"

Amid whinnies, nods, a caw, and a bugle, she said, "Excellent. Here's how I think we should approach them. Let's hear ideas to make mine stronger..."

Voices rose and fell. I added suggestions to the mix. Working together felt right in a way very little else had in my long life. The wolf woofed enthusiastically. Good to have him fully on board, but I'd never had any doubts, not really.

"It's a strong beginning," Delilah said softly.

I squeezed her hand. Indeed it was, and we were only just getting started. A year from now, we'd be stronger, more cohesive. A hundred years hence, no one could stop us. It's rare when a dream comes to life. Thanks to the group scattered around this room, mine not only saw the light of day. It was flourishing.

Somewhere in the castle, a clock struck midnight. I'd been daydreaming, but Aidyrth's call to hunt with her broke through my musings.

"You're welcome to join us," I told Delilah.

She nuzzled my neck. "I will, but I'll ride Aidyrth. That way, I won't hold anyone back."

"Meet in the courtyard," the dragon bugled and shimmered from sight. Of course she'd teleport rather than force her bulk through the castle's hallways and doors.

Roland flew out a window. Dorcha clumped down the stairs. I stopped by the bedroom Delilah had chosen for us to leave my clothing and shift. By the time the wolf padded into the courtyard, Delilah was astride her dragon.

I opened the castle gates—because not all of us had wings—and we raced onto the moors. The night was clear and cold with millions of stars dotting Scotland's skies. I took it as an omen for a shining future.

For all of us.

EPILOGUE

Two *hundred years later, more or less*
Guess I can't resist a few more words. The
Circle didn't exactly take off like a racehorse, but it
grew in fits and starts. We number fifty mages now, and every
assassin job in Europe and the British Isles belongs to us.
Rhiana was correct about no one associating me with James's
demise. His infant daughter came to power years later.
Unfortunately, she made many mistakes and was eventually
driven to abdicate. I always liked her and was sad when she
was forced off the throne. Those who came after her have
been a mixed bag.

Our coffers are overflowing; a small staff serves Inverness
Castle and two other guild houses we've established. Most of
the local serfs reclaimed their lands. Unlike the earl, we've
never charged them rent. Even absent the local farmers, we
needn't have worried about crops or foodstuffs. Grateful
monarchs have kept us well supplied.

I got a jump on hunting down the missing werewolves about a month after freeing the first batch. It still hurts my heart, but most were beyond salvage. They'd lost their minds from starvation and torture. Dorcha and her unicorns put them out of their misery. I brought three survivors home to Inverness Castle. Their healing took years. For a while, they were proud members of the Circle, but for one reason or another, all of them eventually left. Probably, in search of a future where they weren't constantly reminded of their long captivity.

The dragons finally caught up with the Morrigan and slapped her back in her cell in Fire Mountain. Though I hunted Anubis for over fifty years, I never did locate him. My guess was his failed gambit drove him back off-world.

My precious Delilah is still with me, but age is finally taking a toll. Aidyrth and I don't talk about the inevitable, but we know what's coming. She says she'll never bond again, but it's grief talking. I want her to remain in the Circle, bonded or not, even though she and Delilah have reminded me it's a violation of our basic charter.

Not a bridge I have to cross today. Delilah has rallied before. Fae healers are among our ranks, and they're caring for her.

There's not much more to say. Many thanks for being part of the Circle's journey. We're still active in the modern world. Every time you read about a mysterious death—or a bunch of them—it's probably our work. We have new associates. Aye, we're still adding to our ranks. Some older mages have left and returned multiple times. Something about not working alone holds appeal.

Funny since one of my worries was assassins wouldn't

warm to being part of something larger than their own efforts. Silly of me, but you never know how something will shake out until you try.

Delilah just entered my study. Her color is better, and she's moving unaided. I'll leave you now since I want to take her walking in the castle gardens. It's a warm, summer day outside, perfect for her because she won't get cold. Aidyrth will want to take her flying too, so I'll be sure to bring a woolen cape to mitigate the winds aloft.

"What are you doing, darling?" She moved to my desk.

"Finishing our story. Remember? We talked about it."

A smile wreathed her beautiful mouth. "I do. But our story isn't over. Not yet. I don't know what the Fae did, but I feel twenty years younger."

Rising to my feet, I wrapped an arm around her. Together we walked out of the study. The Death shadow that had dogged her was gone. It would return, but for today, and tomorrow, next month, and next year we'd live our lives.

The moment we find ourselves living in is all we ever have. I don't want to regret not making the most out of every single one.

You've reached the end of *Grigori,* last of the Circle of Assassin books. I hope you enjoyed it. Please take a moment to leave a review while it's fresh in your mind.

If you liked this series, you might enjoy my reaper series, Gatekeeper. A sample from book one, *Shadow Reaper,* follows.

BOOK DESCRIPTION: SHADOW REAPER

The dead are restless, and a whole lot less cooperative than they have been. That was true even before I drew the short straw and ended up with Vampire duty.

Since then, Reaping has taken way more time. So much, I'm worried I'll lose all the clients from the career that actually feeds me. I run a small private pilot school. It pays most of the bills and means I don't have to keep regular hours.

Death wants me to remain in one piece. She's bailed me out often enough, she's all but ordered me to find other employment. I just smile and nod after our little talks, and then I climb back into a cockpit.

Our last toe-to-toe didn't go so well. She went and assigned Vampires to me. That's when Reaping turned into a million-hour-a-week job. I can almost hear the Reaper who was stuck with them before, laughing his head off.

I shepherd souls to the other side. Vampires have zero

interest in leaving, but I have a quota to fill. Means I have to trick them, but it didn't work for long. They're onto me. Damn Death, anyway. She painted a target on my back, and now the Vamps are out for blood.

In more ways than one.

CHAPTER ONE, CAIT

The screen on my crappy monitor looked blurrier than usual, but it might have been my vision. No sleep these past few nights had to be taking a toll. I rubbed grit out of my eyes and shut them, promising myself it would only be for a couple of seconds. Then I had to get back to last month's books.

They weren't looking good. I'd spent more on mechanic bills and aviation fuel than I'd made. Big surprise. To teach flying, I have to actually be here. Not off chasing Vampires. A sigh started in my chest and burbled out my mouth before I could stop it. Sighing is for wimps.

I'm more of a take-charge type. Or maybe I'm deluding myself.

A pair of ghosts drifted through the far wall, making a beeline right for me. They were on the youngish side, maybe late forties when their lives had been cut out from under them. I'm a Reaper, and souls who have yet to cross are drawn to me like the proverbial moth to a flame. It's a scent thing, kind of like pheromones, except keyed to crossing the veil rather than for sex.

They say hearing is the last sense to go. Nope. It's smell.

I stood and flapped my hands at the approaching pair. "Find another Reaper. I've been reassigned."

"But we're here," the man protested.

"Here," the woman echoed.

They were only a few feet away. A closer look revealed bullet holes in both their foreheads. Crap. Had they been victimized by another mass murderer?

"Please," the man said. "Winnie and me, we—"

"Nope." I turned both hands palms out. "Determining where you end up is above my pay grade. Sorry you're dead, but telling me how it happened is a waste of your time."

At this point, acting as a conduit was simpler than arguing. I covered the remaining distance between us and opened my arms. The duo didn't require further instructions. They walked into my embrace, first one then the other, more than ready to depart this portion of their existence. As I held them, they passed through me.

My Reaper side channeled the dark forever of death, and a chill I knew all too well shot from my toes to my head. If I'd had any hopes of finishing my bookwork, it just went up in smoke. Or ice chips. Reaping is hard work. There are several of us, but never enough to go around.

Fuck it.

I sat back down. Next I pushed the keyboard aside, folded my arms on my dusty desk, and laid my head on top of them. A fifteen-minute nap would do me wonders. Maybe after I finished the books, I'd clean my office. Customers offered pilots latitude when it came to neatness, but I'm not sure I'd climb into an airplane with someone whose workplace looked quite as down-at-the-heels as mine.

Carrick Sky Sports is located in a small Quonset hut right next to the hangar housing my three planes. The hangar was a whole lot cleaner than my digs, but then so were the planes.

I took care of them. They were my babies. Thoughts of airplanes and Vampires and Reaping whirled through my tired brain before I finally nodded off.

A staunch knock startled me so badly, I nearly tumbled out of my chair. It skidded back a few inches, leaving me fighting not to end up on my ass.

"Cait Carrick?" a deep male voice inquired.

I had yet to get a visual on the speaker. At least he wasn't dead. Their voices lacked resonance.

"Yeah. Um, yes. That would be me." I stuffed my feet under my body and stood, turning until I faced the single door into my office. I'm tall, so tall I'm used to looking down at everyone, including men, but the dude who stood there was at least six foot four, topping me by a good two inches.

Faded Levis encased his long legs. Torn trail runners might have been black once, but they'd faded to gray. A battered leather vest and frayed blue-plaid shirt covered his torso. Fair hair was long enough for him to have gathered it behind his head into a ragged braid. He had an interesting face, all planes and angles with a square chin and sharp cheekbones, but his most unusual feature was his eyes. I suppose they were hazel, but in the light streaming through the door behind him, they glowed like burnished copper.

"Sorry to disturb you." He grinned rakishly. "I tried knocking softer, but you were really out of it."

I swallowed back annoyance. I'd be damned if I'd stand here while a total stranger blithely assessed my physical state.

"And you are?" I raised my eyebrows.

"Liam. Liam Hunter." He glided toward me, hand extended.

Something about him bothered me, but I couldn't home in on what it was. I tucked my hands behind my back. "Sorry," I mumbled, "I've got grease all over me. What can I do for you?"

"They say you're the best flight instructor around." His smile, which had slipped a few notches, bloomed again.

"Who's they?" I winced. I should just have said "thank you" and let it be.

"Why all the pilots down at *The Tailwind*."

It was a small bar and grill at the far end of the airstrip I used. Most days, they served breakfast and lunch. Weekends, they served dinner. While I knew all the local pilots, I wasn't aware they ever talked up my skills. Most of them were pretty old-school. Chauvinistic enough to believe women belonged in the kitchen—or the bedroom—rather than in an airplane.

I'd dealt with a lot of flak a decade ago when I opened my business. Once the guys figured out I wasn't a flash in the pan, they dialed back the harassment but never totally accepted me.

What to do about the dude standing three feet away?

He had an expectant look on his face, as if he'd offered up the aeronautical equivalent of "Open Sesame." If I didn't have so many unpaid bills, I'd have chased him out of my office. On the other hand, I didn't want to share a cockpit with someone who started out on the wrong foot by lying to me.

I pushed my shoulders straighter. If I'd gotten any mileage

out of my nap, it wasn't readily apparent. "Um, look, Mr. Hunter—if that's even your name—the other pilots would never steer business my way. Either you play this again from the top, or we have nothing to talk about."

His smile developed a definite sheepish cast. "That transparent, huh?"

I nodded and waited, too tired to spar with him. Night would fall soon enough, and then I'd be back to herding Vampires. Death wanted them in Hell, but they were a slimy, sleazy lot with a huge investment in remaining on Earth.

There it was. My problem in a nutshell. Their motivation in staying topside was significantly more pressing than my need to move them across the veil. I'd quit if I could, but Reapers are born into Reaping.

And we live for a very long time.

The thought of chasing down Vampires until the moon fell out of the sky depressed the living fuck out of me.

"Ms. Carrick?"

I started. I hadn't exactly forgotten Mr. False Name, but he'd moved away from dead-center on my radar. He kicked the door shut. A surge of magic flickered around him, turning the air as blurry as my monitor had been.

"You're right about me being tired," I told him. "If you're about to cut the crap and tell me who you are and why you're here, we'll both be money ahead."

The angles in his face grew more pronounced, his fingers more elongated, the copper cast to his eyes deeper, shinier.

I narrowed my eyes. "Sidhe or Fae. Am I right?"

"Aye, Ms. Carrick. I'm Daoine Sidhe. Liam is a modernization of my name, and my family name is Warwick." His accent had shifted from pure American to a lilting Irish brogue, or maybe it was Scottish. Never could tell them apart.

Breath hissed through my teeth. At least he'd offered his true name. The teensy jolt I'd gotten from the other one hadn't bothered me this time. "You scarcely need my airplanes. You can teleport."

The corners of his generous mouth twisted into a wry expression. "You know about us?"

No point dancing around what I was. I was certain he knew, and my soul-herding skills were why he was here. "I went to Reaper school. We have to get passing grades before Death turns us loose."

He furled a blond brow. "Fascinating. I had no idea."

"How about if you tell me why you're here? Then you can leave. I have work to do." A quick glance through my single window told me time was about to betray me. Sunset would be in maybe an hour. With it would come the Vampire horde blood-bent on my destruction.

Or my assimilation, to be more precise.

He frowned. "You're about to have company. I shall return later."

Before I could tell him not to bother coming back, the place he'd stood was empty. I could still feel the beat of his soul, but damn if he hadn't vanished before my eyes.

I stared at the door. I might not know Mr. Warwick, but I trusted his paranormal ability. Sure enough, a knock was followed by a swoosh as the door flew open. Kiko Tanaka strode inside, dark hair billowing around her head like a cloud. She's my closest friend, and another pilot when she's not busy being a pharmacist. Her Japanese heritage is evident in her slight figure and dark, almond-shaped eyes.

"Not late, am I?" She grinned at me. It lightened her features and made her look about sixteen.

I must have appeared blank because she added, "Remember? You promised me an under-the-hood check ride."

Heat rose to my cheeks. "Sorry. I didn't exactly forget. But it's okay. I have time."

"Are you sure?" Kiko asked. "You're looking a little ragged around the edges."

"Yeah. I'm sure. I'm good for a check ride." To avoid more commentary about how trashed I appeared, I strode to the board and snapped up keys for the Cessna 172. Like I said, I have three airplanes, a Cessna 152 trainer, the 172, and a Piper Seneca. The Piper is a twin-engine jobbie. It costs me five hundred bucks an hour to keep it in the air, so I rarely fly the old girl. She's left over from when I used to have a contract for air freight runs. Then she made sense because she has a great payload.

I really should sell her, but I don't have the heart. Like I said, the planes are my babies.

We left the Quonset hut with Kiko chattering a mile a minute about a hunky dude she'd met the night before. I kicked back and let her manage the preflight checklist. She's efficient. No wasted motion. She even remembered to grab the cushion that made up for her short arms and legs.

She took the left seat; I settled into the right as she nosed the Cessna out of the hangar. I love the moment when a plane is barreling down a runway, gaining the momentum it needs for its wings to carry it skyward. Once we were upstairs, Kiko tugged a hood over her head and proceeded to follow my instructions using the instrument panel rather than her eyes.

We're both IFR certified, which means instrument flight rules. It's the step that comes after VFR. All pilots have to be able to manage their planes under visual flight rules, or they don't get to fly anything.

Didn't take long before we were circling to land. Kiko did a great job, flared at just the right time, and the plane settled gently to the tarmac, right on the numbers at its eastern end.

"Do you want her back inside?" Kiko asked. Her hood lay across her lap. She'd removed it on our final approach.

I shook my head. "Think I'll take her back up for a bit."

She taxied the plane off the runway and patted my thigh. "If there's anything I can do, just holler."

"Thank you." What I didn't say was that talking about my particular problem wouldn't solve anything. She offered up her logbook, and I initialed our check ride.

"I'll leave a check on your desk," Kiko told me. Pushing the door open, she climbed down. I handed her pillow outside before I switched sides of the plane. She knows what I am, but not about my Vampire-herding assignment. I'm not about to tell her—or anyone else, either.

Magic came out of the closet about fifty years ago, but the presence of supernaturals makes most mortals really uncomfortable. If it had only been one variety, things might have gone smoother, but when it became apparent the dude next door could be a witch or a shifter or a Druid or one of the Fae, a backlash developed.

Humans still aren't certain Vampires are real. The fuckers are masters at hiding the corpses they've drained. And the newly turned ones are kept on a very short leash.

Over time, the friction between mortals and magic had done nothing but grow worse. Lots of anger and hatred on both sides of the fence. This group, Humans Rule, has been a particular thorn in my side. Mostly, I keep a low profile and stay out of everyone's way, though.

I have enough problems without turning into a crusader for magic wielders and our rights.

I nosed the Cessna back into the air, glorying in the feel of the plane as I put her through her paces. She's a good compromise. Light, reasonably fuel efficient—for an airplane —and responsive. The sky to the west lit with what was shaping up to be a glorious sunset. On a whim, I flew into it, chasing the colors across the Olympic Peninsula.

When I finally turned back to the east and set the three-axis autopilot to take me home, I considered how to spend the coming evening. Really only two choices. I could barricade myself into my houseboat on Lake Union.

A fortunate choice of residences since Vampires hate water.

Or I could go hunting. Problem was, I'm about out of tricks. Vampires are very old. Even older than me, for the most part. With age comes shrewdness. Because they all talk with each other in some perversion of telepathy, I can only use a strategy once. They were onto me. It was either come up with something new or lie low.

By the time my wheels kissed the tarmac, I'd come to a decision. I had to have another sit-down with Death. If she wanted to purge Earth of Vampires, maybe she had some ideas—other than driving the Reaper assigned to them nuts. The guy before me had done pretty much nothing. It's not like Death can fire us.

I considered my options as I taxied off the runway and into my hangar. I could follow the other Reaper's example, but it went against the grain. I'm not lazy. Beyond that, I do not like to lose. At anything.

Right now, I was slightly ahead. Majorly ahead, actually. I'd shunted an even dozen Vamps to their rightful spot, presumably in Hell. The way it works is this. I'm a gateway, a link between Earth and Death's domain. The dead pass through me, but I have no jurisdiction over their destination.

Better if I don't know.

I can't imagine a Vampire ending up in the good spot, though.

I buttoned up the plane and pulled the hangar door shut. It creaked on its rollers, and I added spraying them with silicone to my endless to-do list. Once the hangar was locked, I trotted to the Quonset hut. I was feeling better. Flying always lifted my spirits.

And I had a direction scoped out. My next heart-to-heart with Death had to happen soon. I'd make some notes, to be sure I didn't miss anything, and then I'd reach out to her.

It was full dark when I unlocked my office and walked through the door, clicking on the overheads as I passed the bank of switches. I returned the Cessna's keys to their hook on the board. Kiko's money was dead center on my desk. If I hadn't been so cash-strapped, I'd have told her the check ride was on the house, but av gas wasn't cheap. Last week it topped six bucks a gallon, and we'd burned through seventy dollars' worth before my solo indulgence flight.

My monitor had long since blacked out as my computer went into sleep mode. I considered returning to my bookwork but didn't feel like it. The bad news would hold till tomorrow. Even without hard figures, I had choices to make. Either I freed up enough time to make *Carrick Sky Sports* profitable again, or I'd have to sell my planes. Hangar rent was two thousand dollars a month. Upkeep on the planes another thousand—if I was lucky.

Normally, it was doable. Flight lessons were expensive. And I could always bid to fly freight with the Piper Seneca again. But to do those things, I needed time. And a decent night's sleep every night. Not sleeping because I was on Vampire patrol was the linchpin that was killing me.

I rolled my eyes. What an unfortunate turn of phrase. I was only about six months into Vampire patrol, and I was sick of it.

Maybe thinking about the Undead drew them, but the lights flickered, and the chill of grave dirt descended on my head like a ton of bricks. Thank all the gods I had a moment's warning. It was enough for me to dash to the locker where I keep my street clothes and grab the saber I'd bought for just these occasions.

It had cost me an obscene amount of money, but the blade is a mix of silver and iron. Perfect for unruly Vamps and not quite as personal as impaling them through the heart with silver stakes. This way, the length of the blade is between us. Stakes would have required me to be right up next to the loathsome fuckers.

I swung the blade, ready for damn near anything. I'd taken a few lessons in swordsmanship once I bought the saber. Those were a bitch to find. It's not the Middle Ages anymore. Not too many knights errant wandering about running schools for wanna-be warriors.

My death-sense intensified. The smell of rot pervaded my office. Could they come in without an invitation? The lore suggested otherwise, but I'd run across the occasional

Vampire in broad daylight, so the rulebook didn't seem to apply any longer.

Sure enough, one sashayed through a wall. I didn't bother looking at him. They're all hunks. And they all reek of decay. Another followed him. And another, until half a dozen formed a semicircle around me. I'd been savvy enough to place a wall behind me, or I'd have been surrounded.

Smart fuckers. They understood my blade would end them, so they kept just beyond its path. I glared. They glared back. Every time I made a move, they jumped nimbly out of my way. They're fast. Superhuman speed and strength comes along with the blood-spell that turns them.

Dawn might end my predicament, but I did not want to spend the next nine hours staring down the maw of a Vampire horde. More were joining the ones already here. Naturally. A telepathic summons must have gone out. My throat was dry, my breathing shallow. They'd planned this, probably just been waiting for a night when I was stupid enough to be in my office after the sun went down.

I raised my mind voice and shrieked, *"Death!"*

"She can't help you." A blond who could have been a cover model for GQ leered at me.

"You'll like us. Once you're one of us." A woman with long russet hair smiled, displaying her fangs.

Yeah. That is so not going to happen. I can't teleport, though. The floor wasn't about to open up and swallow me. If I charged forward, blade swinging, I might behead a few, but not before one of them sank his fangs into my neck.

I've been in bad spots before, but not quite this difficult. Better to go down fighting than cowering, though. With a pivot in what I hoped was an unexpected direction, I drove the point of my saber through a Vampire chest. It wasn't a silver stake, but it should work the same way.

The Vampire shuddered and collapsed. Where its body had been was a pile of moldering bones. I didn't even have to bother freeing my blade. The circle around me backed up a foot or so.

My breath came in ragged pants. I swung about and skewered another one. This Vamp was younger. Blood spurted from it, blackish ichor that outdid any charnel pit for stink.

Motion from the corner of my eye was the only warning I got. Swinging blind, I beheaded the Vamp trying to close on me from one side. Bones clattered as he hit the floor.

They could do this all night. I couldn't. I was already woozy from six months of barely sleeping. Where was Death? She'd always come before when I called her. I'm a Reaper, not a soldier. Reaping is usually peaceful.

I silenced my mind. Feeling sorry for myself—or expecting help to materialize—were dead ends. At least it was late enough, no mortals were likely to show up. I didn't want to be the cause of anyone joining the ranks of the Undead.

Time passed. I stabbed, swung, stabbed some more. My head hurt. My hands hurt. My eyes were giving me trouble, refusing to focus. I can build wards, but not against the dead. It would be counterproductive since I'm supposed to be a beacon for them.

A burst of furious Old Gaelic battered my ears. Great. A Celtic Vampire. Just peachy. Had this bunch summoned the Undead version of someone like Sir Lancelot? I narrowed my eyes, but my vision was a joke. Blurry and caught up in the half-light common to the dead, I couldn't see a thing.

"Move over, Ms. Carrick," a familiar voice ordered just

before a man slinging magic burst through a portal. I blinked against the glare arcing from his fingers.

"Liam?"

"Who in the bloody fuck did you expect? Santa Claus?" Intent on beheading Vamps with Sidhe magic, he didn't so much as glance my way.

I admit, I was slow on the uptake, but once it sank in I might not end up turned tonight, I waded into the fray, swinging my saber with renewed energy. Maybe Liam did something, but my lethargy dropped away. Once I had enough oomph to drag all of me back to the land of the living, my vision returned to normal.

My mind was firing on all cylinders again, and I didn't care for its conclusions. Liam wanted something. He must have wanted it pretty damned bad to show up now. Surely, his Sidhe magic told him what he was walking into.

I was grateful, sure I was, but also suspicious as hell. Why did I have the feeling death by Vampire might be preferable to the favor Liam was about to call in?

Tough to refuse someone who'd just saved my bacon. Tough, but not impossible. I cautioned myself to wait. Once we were out of this, I'd keep as open a mind as possible. At least listen to him before I said no.

Keep right on reading. Click here for information and buy links.

ABOUT THE AUTHOR

Ann Gimpel is a USA Today bestselling author. A lifelong aficionado of the unusual, she began writing speculative fiction a few years ago. Since then her short fiction has appeared in many webzines and anthologies. Her longer books run the gamut from urban fantasy to paranormal romance. Once upon a time, she nurtured clients. Now she nurtures dark, gritty fantasy stories that push hard against reality. When she's not writing, she's in the backcountry getting down and dirty with her camera. She's published over 100 books to date, with several more planned for 2023 and beyond. A husband, grown children, grandchildren, and wolf hybrids round out her family.

Keep up with her at https://www.anngimpel.com or https://www.anngimpelaudiobooks.com

If you enjoyed what you read, get in line for special offers and pre-release special reads. Newsletter Signup!

ALSO BY ANN GIMPEL

SERIES

Alphas in the Wild

Hello Darkness

Alpine Attraction

A Run for Her Money

Fire Moon

Bitter Harvest

Deceived

Twisted

Abandoned

Betrayed

Redeemed

Cataclysm

Harsh Line

Warped Line

Cracked Line

Broken Line

Circle of Assassins

Shira

Quinn

Rhiana

Alice's Alphas

Megan's Mates

Sophie's Shifters

Wylde Magick

Gemstone

Lion's Lair

Unbalanced

STANDALONE BOOKS

Branded, That Old Black Magic Romance (paranormal romance)

Edge of Night (short story collection, paranormal and horror)

Grit is a 4-Letter Word (nonfiction)

Heart's Flame (post-apocalyptic romance)

Icy Passage (science fiction romance)

Marked by Fortune (post-apocalyptic coming of age story)

Melis's Gambit (historical paranormal romance)

Midnight Magic (paranormal romance)

Red Dawn (post-apocalyptic paranormal romance)

Shadow Play (historical paranormal romance)

Shadows in Time (Highland time travel romance)

Since We Fell (contemporary romance)

Warin's War (paranormal romance)

CPSIA information can be obtained
at www.ICGtesting.com
Printed in the USA
LVHW052135301222
736235LV00034B/1342